TARGETED BY THE SEAL

HERO FORCE BOOK SIX

AMY GAMET

1

_____

It was the scent of dew heavy on the crisp morning air that first registered on Austin Dixon's senses. The fact that he wasn't dead, the second.

So fucking cold.

His eyes were closed, the lids too heavy to open, and his teeth chattered. His body was seemingly suspended in air, making him wonder if he wasn't dead after all.

The weeping pain in his skull seemed to expand against the bone. Alive, then. He worked to feel his limbs, fighting a deep-seated fatigue that immobilized his muscles, straining for the slightest movement of his feet. He knew what was wrong with him.

Hypothermia. He was freezing to death.

Where the hell was he? He tried to remember the last thing he'd been doing, but only emptiness met his efforts. The wind blew cold with a whistling howl and a bird squawked in the distance.

Wake up, asshole, or you're going to be food for the vultures.

It took every bit of energy he had to open his eyes, the

brightness focusing the pain in his head to a fine, brutal point.

A tree?

Evergreen branches surrounded him in pale pink light, his body hanging down and his feet dangling beneath him. God only knew how high up he was.

"Shit."

He twisted his neck, noting the stiffness that told him he'd been in that position far too long. There above him were paracords that held him suspended, a crumpled parachute higher in the tree, his memory instantly returning.

Cassidy.

Air rushed by his body as he fell through the sky. He'd made hundreds of jumps in his career and hundreds more for recreation, though this was the kind that really got his blood pumping. Two in the morning and pitch-black, his night vision goggles throwing the world into an eerie green.

Logan and Noah were right behind him, the three of them falling toward the Sawtooth Mountains at breakneck speed.

The landing zone was a small clearing in the dense forest which would require careful turns after chute deployment, and Austin kept an eye on the other divers' locations to be sure he had the clearance he needed to make those turns.

Noah was an experienced skydiver, but Logan only had forty or fifty jumps under his belt, with this being his third one in darkness. The night vision goggles were bulky and took a lot of getting used to. The ones they'd used as SEALs had four tubes to allow a greater range of vision, but the HERO Force sets had only two.

The effect was like looking through toilet paper rolls,

and it could be unnerving when you were also falling through the sky.

He checked his altimeter, having chosen manual chute deployment instead of automatic for this jump. They were too close together for a one-size-fits-all answer, and Austin liked to keep as much control as possible. He pulled his ripcord, slowing his rapid descent to a gentle ride.

Then something went wrong.

He started to spin and he looked up to see his canopy partially uninflated. Noah must have clipped him with his legs. He tried to self-correct but the spin only intensified. He needed to cut his main chute loose and deploy his reserve, but if Logan was directly above him Austin's chute could become entangled in his.

A more experienced skydiver would see Austin was in trouble and get out of the way, but he could no longer see Logan and didn't know if that's what Doc had done.

He could only rely on best practices and hope Logan had done what he was supposed to do. He cut away his main chute— all too aware of the numbers flashing by on his altimeter—and deployed his reserve.

It should have solved his problem, but it did not. Now he was spinning in the opposite direction. He must have collided with Logan again. He was going down, the tree-covered ground approaching much too quickly. He worked to control his descent as best he could but the results were futile.

He crashed into a tree and blacked out.

That explained how he got here. Now where the fuck was everybody else?

He was worried. More than worried. Skydiving accidents were rare, but canopy collisions were all too frequently the cause and just as often, unsurvivable. He'd been lucky to land in the tree as he had, and he could only hope his friends had been just as fortunate.

He activated the com set in his helmet. "Logan, you copy?"

No answer.

"Cowboy?"

There was only the blowing breeze.

He tried several more times, his mind considering what had likely caused the accident and how that might have affected Noah's landing.

It could be bad. Really bad.

He gave up on the headset. "I'm fucking talking to myself."

He needed to cut himself down, but the way his legs were feeling that would be like cutting a dead man from the gallows. He slowly pulled his knees up to his chest, forcing blood into the muscles once more despite the pain. He pumped his arms as his mind returned to their mission.

I have to get to Cassidy.

He thought of what it must have cost her father to look him up. Senator Keaton Lane had gone to extremes to keep Austin out of his daughter's life. The fact that he had sought him out now told Austin just how dire the situation really was.

An investigative journalist in Washington, Cassidy had told her family she was going to Paris for a much-needed vacation, but when her parents checked up on her they found she'd never left the country.

After calling in a favor from the CIA to access their daughter's email, the senator and his wife learned Cassidy had joined The Community—a group of more than two hundred people living high in the Idaho mountains under the direction of a man named David Kelleher.

Her parents immediately checked with Cassidy's boss at the paper, who insisted he hadn't sent her, but told them another journalist from the *Post* had gone missing after entering The Community several months earlier.

Cassidy's best friend, Julianne Garrison.

That was bad enough, but when Senator Lane's eyes met Austin's across the table and he told him Julianne's bloodied press credentials had been delivered to the *Washington Post* in yesterday's mail—along with a necklace she always wore — Austin started to pace the conference room like a caged animal.

Julianne was dead and Cassidy—*his Cassidy*—was in trouble.

It took HERO Force two days to prepare for the mission, time in which Austin thought he might lose his goddamn mind.

Community leader Kelleher had grown up on the four thousand acre Longwood Ranch that was now home base for The Community, inheriting the property from his parents when they were killed in a farming accident years earlier. His parents were potato farmers with a small herd of cattle, but Longwood Ranch no longer sold any goods.

It was a dot on the map of a sparsely populated area that most people wouldn't even know existed. The perfect place for a crazy motherfucker to set up shop unnoticed.

Satellite images showed Longwood Ranch was a world unto itself. A world full of potentially dangerous isolationists in an extensive, self-supporting compound surrounded by a razor-wire-topped fence and two guard towers—and somewhere inside, a senator's daughter who may or may not want to come home. There was a series of buildings close to the main house as well as several outlying structures that had likely once been used for crop storage and machinery.

He thought of the picture Cassidy's mother had pushed across the conference table with her trembling hand and perfectly manicured fingernails, Austin suddenly feeling like he'd been sucker-punched. Cassidy wore a slim skirt and slightly open blouse, her dark hair tucked behind one ear and her green eyes laughing at the camera.

She'd only gotten more beautiful in the years since he last saw her. She was an ivy league girl with the world in her hands, who clearly came from money and swam in the waters of opportunity.

Whereas you grew up running through the spray of fire hydrants in Brooklyn.

That was only part of the problem.

His mind was off and running, the photograph taking him back in time until she was beneath him in the grass, her naked body open to him and her legs wrapped around his hips, the scent of flowers and summer breezes surrounding him as he pumped into her sweet body.

"Cassidy would do anything to make sure Julianne was okay," said her mother. Her voice broke, and her husband took her hand.

"I'll find her," said Austin. "You can count on me."

The senator met his eyes with a soulful look. "Yes. I believe you will."

That was why they came to him, he could see now. He'd been useless to them then—someone to be looked down upon—but now his passion for their daughter could work to their advantage.

It doesn't matter. That's all in the past.

"There's something else," said the senator, glancing at his wife's worried face. She nodded. The senator turned and stared hard at Cowboy. "It's classified information. I could go to jail for telling you this, but I am a father before I am a congressman."

Cowboy nodded. "Go ahead."

"My contact at the CIA tells me The Community is planning to attack a major city five days from today. The CIA is going to raid the compound, but Cassidy..." His throat worked and his stare went to each member of the HERO Force team, one by one. "They can't guarantee her safety. You have to get her out of there before anything happens. I'm trusting you with her life."

Memories haunted Austin on the flight from Atlanta, along with the image of a smiling Cassidy in his mind. He'd even dreamed about her, his head bouncing against the window of the plane as he touched her skin after so many years without her.

"Stop it," he said out loud, forcing his attention back to the present. Blood was flowing through his extremities, and while that intensified the pain, it showed progress. His muscles were contracting at will. He was still weak, but that would only get worse unless he could get himself out of this tree and moving around. He reached into the pocket of his tactical vest and withdrew a knife.

He made a sign of the cross, a habit ingrained from his childhood and one of a hundred things Cassidy's father probably hated about him. "Here goes nothing." He cut the cords that held him and fell through twenty feet of branches on his way to the ground. His vision jerked and shook with the impact that knocked the wind out of his lungs.

The pack on his back was heavy—some sixty pounds—and he circled his stiff shoulder backwards as he unbuckled the strap. He opened the pack and withdrew a map. He had no way of knowing where Noah and Logan were, or if they were even alive. They'd been separated at a high enough altitude and with enough force that the other men could be a quarter mile or more in any direction. One or both of them might have bounced—a not-so-accurate description of hitting the ground at an unsurvivable speed.

He could only focus on Cassidy now. She was in danger and he might be the only member of HERO Force who was close enough to do anything about it. They were down to three days until The Community attacked and he needed to get her out of harm's way.

There wasn't enough time for him to hike out of these woods and make it back to HERO Force in time to regroup and try again. He'd have to go in after her alone. That woman needed somebody on her side, and he was it.

He unfolded the map, quickly locating their intended drop zone. He was sure he was near it, just a mile and a half from Longwood Ranch and The Community to his north. With his concussion, hypothermia and muscle fatigue, he'd be hard-pressed to make it there by nightfall.

But he would make it.

Nighttime would be the perfect opportunity to infiltrate the perimeter. He withdrew his compass and kissed the glass face his father had given him when he made Eagle Scout, just weeks before the old man died.

He set out toward the compound, a plan taking shape in his mind. His mission wouldn't be as simple as it would have been with Doc and Noah by his side, but Austin was confident he could get inside the compound and find Cassidy on his own.

Hell, he'd better be confident.

There was no other way.

2

Longwood Ranch reminded Cassidy of a resort her parents had taken her to when she was younger. Every detail of the log-cabin-type structures screamed farmhouse chic—from the exposed wooden beams of the dining hall, carefully wrapped in tiny white lights, to the early-American artifacts and artwork on every surface and wall of each building.

It was beautiful here, with a warm safe feeling she knew was ironic. She'd yet to find any clue as to Julianne's where-abouts, or even confirmation that her friend had been in this place. If Cassidy revealed she was looking for her, she would be in danger herself.

It was important she be discreet.

Her eyes swept from one end of the dining hall to the other, scanning the faces of the people who were slowly becoming her friends as they chatted with each other and enjoyed their meal. Steely eyes connected with hers across the room, stopping her perusal and freezing her thoughts.

Thomas.

A shiver went down her spine as she dropped her gaze.

Something about that man unnerved her. He always seemed to be questioning, as if he could see through her facade and knew she wasn't here simply because she longed to live in harmony with others. Given that he was David's right-hand man, he could be a serious problem.

She longed to stare Thomas down or put him in his place with an icy, "Can I help you?" but she bit her tongue. She picked up her wineglass and took a sip of strawberry wine, the overly sweet liquid making her stomach clench.

"Are you enjoying your meal?" asked David.

"It's delicious." She forced a small smile in his direction. He'd insisted she eat beside him yesterday and today, claiming he wanted to get to know her. While she initially thought she'd roused his suspicion, she'd since become certain she'd roused something else entirely. David Kelleher was interested in her, and he was making a point of demonstrating it in front of the whole community.

He of all people knew what happened to Julianne, and Cassidy planned to take full advantage of his interest in her to find out what he knew. She just needed to keep a safe distance between them.

And if you can't?

He was looking at her like the Big Bad Wolf come to eat her up, and her stomach seemed to cave in, her shoulders rounding as if she'd been punched. She took another sip of wine.

Back in her real life, she could take care of herself with her sharp wit and—if it came to it— her self-defense skills. But this was a different situation entirely. She was living in a commune of people who believed the man beside her talked to God, who came far too close to worshipping the ground he walked on.

How could she defend herself from that?

A wave of fatigue crested over her. Her back hurt from bending over in the field all day, her hands sore from working without gloves, and her soul already tired of pretending.

David refilled her wine.

She couldn't help the sardonic tone to her voice. "You seem to think alcohol improves the quality of my company."

"It needs no improvement."

That's because I'm pretending to be a doormat, you asshole.

She stifled any opinions that were not in agreement with his and nodded enthusiastically when he spoke to the group. In the time she'd been here, she'd already decided he was an egotistical sociopath who needed to be stroked and coddled.

"I like you as you are, Sister Cassidy."

He touched her leg beneath the table and she jerked away, instantly regretting the automatic reaction. She needed him to believe she liked him. "I don't really know you," she said.

"You know everything that matters. You know I love this community and my country, and I'll defend them both until the day I die."

"That isn't what I mean." She looked at her hands in her best imitation of a demure woman.

"Ask me anything, then."

"Have you ever been married?"

"No."

"Why did you start The Community?"

"I was called to in a dream. The archangel Raphael appeared to me and told me what I should do."

She narrowed her eyes. "Do you talk to angels a lot?"

"Yes."

"And you talk to God?"

"Only on Fridays and Wednesday afternoons."

"Seriously?"

He laughed. "No, not seriously. You ask too many questions. Walk with me after dinner."

"Sure. Do people ever leave The Community?"

The shift in his demeanor was so subtle, she might have missed it. "No. Everyone here has taken a vow to remain part of the group for the rest of their lives. If you choose to stay with us more than a few more days, you'll need to make your vow as well."

Over my dead body.

"What if someone who's taken their vow wants to leave?"

"That doesn't happen."

"But what if—"

He held up his hand. "No buts."

"Does that mean everyone who's ever been to The Community is still here now?"

He cocked his head to the side. "Why do you ask these things?"

Cassidy wished she could backpedal. She'd pushed him too much and roused his suspicions. She shrugged. "I'm just curious."

"Are you finished with your meal, Sister Cassidy?" She turned to find Lucas, David's personal helper, standing behind her. He'd been kind to her since she first arrived and she smiled warmly.

"Yes, thank you. Everything was wonderful." She turned back around to find David looking at her intently.

"I have a few questions for you, too," he said.

Crap. "Okay."

"What do you do for a living?"

She'd invented a completely fake persona to rely on when questioned. "I'm a schoolteacher. Fourth grade."

"Where do you live?"

"Virginia, outside D.C."

"Ever been married?"

"No."

"Have you been with a man?"

Her mouth dropped open, blood instantly rushing to her cheeks. "Excuse me?"

"The answer to that question says a lot about a woman's character. Have you let a man lie with you out of wedlock?"

She'd never wanted to tell anyone off so badly in her life, but the sweet little schoolteacher she'd invented for this occasion probably wouldn't do that. She forced her mouth closed but didn't trust herself to answer him.

He stroked up and down her thigh. "Now I've upset you."

She yanked her leg away. "I don't think I'd like to walk this evening, after all."

"Be very careful, Sister Cassidy."

The hair on her arms stood up on end. Was this what had happened to Julianne? Had she made David angry? Had he hurt her?

She stood abruptly and pushed her chair in.

"I'll call on you around eight," he said.

She didn't trust herself not to stay in control, so she turned on her heel and left, weaving her way in and out of the others who were leaving the dining hall.

She was suddenly certain this place wasn't what it seemed. It couldn't just be people living together and working in harmony.

The Community had lured Julianne in and closed around her like a Venus flytrap, her disappearing just as surely as a fly in that same predicament. Was the same thing going to happen to her?

You've been lazy, waiting for answers to come to you. You must explore the compound. See for yourself where Julianne might be.

It would be dangerous, but she saw now it was something she must do. David wasn't just going to tell her what happened to her friend. She would have to find out for herself.

3

I f she doesn't want to leave, you're going to have to drag her out, kicking and screaming.

Austin thought it with every step as he hiked up the mountain to Longwood Ranch. If he'd learned anything during his weeks with Cassidy Lane, it was that woman had a skull even thicker than his own, and damn the person who tried to argue with her.

He could only hope once she learned about the press pass and the necklace, she'd understand her friend was gone and she herself was in danger, but somehow he imagined she wouldn't concede a damn thing without a body and a coroner to pronounce Julianne dead beyond saving.

Maybe she'd grown up by now and wasn't so damn stubborn. He imagined she'd throw her arms around him and thank him for coming to his rescue.

He scoffed out loud.

He had drugs in his pack he could use to knock Cassidy out if necessary. He'd probably have to carry her down the whole damn mountain against her will, but he'd be lying if he said the task didn't sound more than a little like fun.

Even if she wouldn't fight for me.

The old resentment bubbled up through layers of forgotten memories. Since Cassidy's parents came to visit HERO Force, he'd been swimming in the moments he'd shared with their daughter, from the most intense love-making to the final argument that had ended it all.

Austin spit on the ground and climbed up a small cliff. He wasn't a dreamer and he never expected she'd come back into his life. But he was on a journey to bring her to safety, and with every step he secured that destiny as surely as if he were flying cross-country to meet her.

Again.

He'd been such a fool. A one-night stand had turned into a weekend, a weekend into seventeen days of the most intense lust and most comfortable lounging in bed together he'd experienced to this day.

He'd been on leave from the SEALs. She'd been on break from college. Neither of them had anything to do beyond strip naked and fuck until their bodies were nearly raw from the friction and his soul sated beyond belief.

Austin had found something in Cassidy he'd never found in another woman before or since. A true partner, a lover and a confidant.

Then all hell had broken loose.

He thought of her father sitting across the HERO Force conference table, still looking regal despite the years that had collected at his feet since Austin had seen him last. The only time he'd seen Senator Keaton Lane even remotely weary was when he stumbled upon his daughter riding Austin on the diving board of the family pool like a jockey in the last stretch at the Kentucky Derby.

It'll be okay, I promise.

But it wasn't okay. Not that day when he got dressed and shook her father's hand, and not a week later when he flew in before going wheels up with SEAL Team Fourteen just to tell her he loved her.

It would never be okay again.

She let him go, just like that. As if none of it meant anything to her.

We're from different worlds, Austin. I know you understand.

He understood, all right. He understood her father was calling the shots and Cassidy was letting him. She was a fighter—that much was clear—but she'd chosen not to fight for the guy a dozen spots beneath her on the social totem pole.

It was going to be a pleasure to pull her out of that compound, even against her will. To make her do what was best for her even if she didn't want it. The fact that all of this was at her father's bidding was just the icing on the cake, karma come full circle to bite Cassidy on the ass.

He frowned at the direction his thoughts had taken.

So much for being over her.

He stopped walking and checked his compass, then continued, slightly adjusting his course. It was beginning to get dark and he needed to setup camp near Longwood Ranch before he stopped moving for the night.

He looked around him. How the hell did they get people in and out of this place, much less supplies? Air was the only reasonable answer, but that was expensive.

He shed his first layer of clothing, tucking the fabric neatly into his pack and retrieving his canteen, taking a long pull of water before moving again.

From here he could see the mountain rise up before him, its majestic peaks arranged in a jagged sawtooth pattern, which was where they'd gotten their name, the Sawtooth Mountains.

You're not in Brooklyn anymore.

The first time he'd thought that he'd been trudging through Tel Aviv. Ever since then, whenever he saw or experienced something extraordinary - whether good or bad - those same words ran through his mind.

You're not in Brooklyn anymore.

That was part of the reason he'd signed up in the first place, the navy seeming like some magical ticket that could transform his life and experiences—hell, even himself—into something beyond brownstones and the same life everyone around him led.

He wanted adventure. He wanted to see things, do things that other people didn't get to see and do.

He grabbed onto a tree trunk and pulled himself up a steep incline. The brush underfoot had given way to pine needles and dirt, the terrain quickly becoming more rugged.

This was what he lived for now. The ever-changing adventure that constantly surprised him, the scenery unlike anything the old Austin could have dreamed.

He was proud to be military, even if now he was collecting a pension instead of a paycheck. It wasn't hard to get the time in when you started early enough, and he'd always be a SEAL even without the active duty.

HERO Force seemed like a good fit so far, keeping him interested with a variety of assignments and enough clandestine missions to keep him interested and challenged.

The watchtower came into view before anything else, rising above the forest like the spire of the castle. There was plenty of cover here, and he moved stealthily from tree to tree without difficulty. By the time he approached the less-vegetated area that separated him from the compound, he was ready for the necessary break.

He'd wait until sundown to gain entry to the compound and find Cassidy. And God willing, get her the hell out of there.

4

David Kelleher stood on his porch and sipped at his honey whiskey. The sun was setting over the mountain, the sky streaked with purple and red. The kind of sky his mother would have called heaven sent, and gone on to talk about how lucky they were to live in the mountains of Idaho.

He liked them much better without her here. His father, too. The day they died was his emancipation, the start of something better and his own kingdom atop the hill. It was good they were gone. When they were alive, they'd spent their meager earnings from the farm on flying to private therapist appointments for their son's delusions of grandeur.

Stupid people.

He tossed back the rest of his drink, the cloyingly sweet liquor what he considered to be Bacchus' nectar of the gods.

His birthright to drink it up.

In his mind's eye he could see Cassidy as she tried to drink it down, the image colliding with an equally appealing fantasy of her giving him oral sex. He liked the new girl—even more than Julianne—and that was saying something.

The thought of his betrayer made him sneer.

Fucking reporter.

He'd worked tirelessly to build The Community into what it was today, poised on the verge of mass adoption, and that bitch had nearly ruined everything. Thank goodness for the tip he'd received that warned him of her true identity before it was too late to stop her from exposing Longwood Ranch and his followers.

He needed her to disappear. It had been a difficult order to give, his desire for the woman and his need to punish her warring in his mind until good sense had finally prevailed.

Now Julianne was dead, but Cassidy was very much alive. She certainly seemed like an honest soul, but hadn't Julianne seemed like one, too?

Touching her at dinner had gotten him hard, the soft firmness of her thigh and the uncomfortable way she tossed her hair. He smiled. She'd been flustered, and he liked his women flustered when he took them to bed. Too willing and it sucked some of the fun from the experience. He needed that uncertainty in order to have something to conquer. A branch to bend, an arm to twist backwards.

He thought back to her reaction when he asked if she'd been with a man. She'd been shocked, certainly. But he didn't think he'd be so lucky as for her to actually be a virgin. In this day and age, people had no sense of sexual morals, no reason to hold off pleasure today for a greater pleasure tomorrow. The idea of saving yourself for your future husband was considered antiquated and unnecessary.

Not for long.

The Community was going to change all that.

Longwood Ranch was its own little world, a sample of the larger society, proving his ideals could survive on a grand scale if given the chance. Like a seed sown in ready soil, his community would flourish in the wider world. He needed only to till that soil and destroy the weeds that currently covered the earth with sinners and non-believers so his doctrine could take root.

Then there would be virgins for any righteous husband, ripe for the picking.

Or breaking, as the case may be.

Thomas walked onto the porch, Lucas on his heels.

"What have you learned about Cassidy?" David asked.

Lucas looked to Thomas before speaking, continuing only after the other man gave a nod. "Cassidy Lane is a schoolteacher from Richmond, Virginia. She's never been married. Her parents are deceased and she's an only child."

So she'd been telling the truth. He grinned as he walked to a table and poured himself more honey whiskey. "Gentlemen, I believe I have found the woman I will marry."

"Perhaps in time," said Thomas.

David spun to face him at the blatant insubordination. "I decide when. Not you, and you're not entitled to an opinion in this matter. Unless of course God has been whispering in your ear without telling me?"

Thomas looked suddenly pale. "Of course not, Brother David. Only you have the ear of the Lord."

"That's right." He turned to Lucas. "Good work, man."

"Thank you, Brother David."

David looked back to Thomas, defying the other man to contradict his next words. "I will have her before we take down Seattle."

Thomas's eyes registered no emotion. "As you wish, Brother David."

"Good. How is the training going?"

"Very well, sir. The men have truly taken to the assault rifles. They believe they are for hunting."

"They are lambs who must become bulls. First we teach them the skills, then we plant the desire to proselytize. Only when I say so will the transformation begin."

"As you wish," said Thomas.

"Brother David?" asked Lucas, his brows knitted together. "Should we pray for the people of Seattle, that they may find conversion before it is too late?"

The earnest expression in Lucas's eyes filled David with pity for this man who thought anyone was worth saving. "No, Brother Lucas. It is already too late for them."

He finished his drink and slammed the glass down. "I have courting to do, gentlemen." He turned on his heel. Cassidy no longer wished to go for a walk with him, but that was no deterrent to his plan.

She would accompany him. She would walk anywhere he wished to walk, and she would like it.

5

Cassidy stepped outside with David, the cool evening air instantly chilling her arms.

"You're cold," he said.

"No. It feels good."

"I can get you a jacket."

"No, really. I'd just like to see the garden and get back." Again with that smile locked onto her face. She swore, if she ever got out of this place she'd never smile again. They walked in silence past the other dormitories and his residence.

Would he kiss her? The thought was sobering, the idea of his hands on her body akin to being covered with spiders, and she shook her head to clear the image.

"I've enjoyed having you here at The Community," he said.

"As I've enjoyed being here."

"Not just as a member of the group, Cassidy. I've enjoyed having you here as a man enjoys having a beautiful woman nearby."

His hand touched hers and she pulled away, crossing her arms over her chest as she walked.

"Is something wrong?" he asked.

Doormat. Be a doormat, Cassidy!

She clenched her teeth to keep from telling him off. She'd been flabbergasted when he showed up at her dorm after dinner, asking for this walk after she'd specifically told him she didn't want to walk with him. But several women were standing nearby and she suspected it was wiser to go with him than to challenge him in front of their audience.

Now they were alone, some five hundred feet from the nearest building, and she used her best diplomatic voice, the one she reserved for her father's cocktail parties and the drunken old politicians who'd stare at her cleavage.

"I told you I didn't want to walk this evening," she said quietly. "But you came for me anyway. You put me in a difficult position."

"I told you at dinner I would be by to collect you. It shouldn't have been a surprise."

"You ignored my wishes."

"I wanted to spend time with you."

She sighed heavily. "Where are the gardens you wanted to show me?"

"Just ahead. Near the fence over there."

Cassidy couldn't even make out a fence in the near darkness. She'd never been to this area of the ranch and it struck her that if she wanted to find Julianne, she needed to cover more territory than the dormitories, fields and dining hall. "I'd like to see more of the ranch. Would it be all right if I looked around tomorrow instead of helping with the planting? I'd like to see the rest of the property."

"Of course. I'll have Lucas take you on a tour."

"There's no need. I can look around myself."

"It's four thousand acres. More than six square miles."

Disappointment pierced her heart. She'd never find Julianne in that much space. "Okay then, Lucas it is."

They walked a few more minutes in silence, then he stopped and lifted his head, calling, "Jerome, will you light the garden, please?"

She could just make out the silhouette of the guard tower against the sky when a large spotlight was lighted, burning her eyes and forcing her to turn away. It moved to the ground, illuminating a large round labyrinth made of gravel and sand. She stepped closer, amazed. "Oh."

"You didn't think it would be a flower garden at this time of year."

"I don't know what I thought. But this is...unexpected." She began at the opening, following the twisting, turning path as it folded in on itself, leading to the middle of the circle.

"I find it easier to speak to God in the garden," he said.

A tingle went up her spine. Not until this moment had she considered David might be telling the truth about his visions and conversations with angels. It was unnerving either way—lying or telling the truth.

"He told me you were coming," he said.

She stopped abruptly and turned to him. "What?"

He moved to the opening of the maze, tracing her steps and following her through that quadrant until he stood before her, the spotlight shining on his face. He touched her cheek. "God told me to expect you. A woman created just for me, untouched by other men."

She was about as far from a virgin as a woman could get, and she stifled a laugh.

If you only knew the half of it, buddy.

She was holding her breath, and she forced herself to breathe. "How do you know he was talking about me?"

He grabbed both her upper arms, startling her. "Because I know. He told me she would be an outsider, and she would come to me from the city. I was confused at first when another outsider came to us this winter. I thought she must be the one, but I was mistaken."

Julianne?

"What did she look like?" The question was out of her mouth before she considered he might find it strange.

"The devil."

"What was her name?"

A movement in her peripheral vision caught her attention and she turned toward it. The space between the outside fence and the inner compound was empty, and she furrowed her brow.

David didn't seem to notice. "I thought she was someone she was not. When I got to know her better I realized she'd been sent to distract me from my mission."

"Someone from The Community? Is she still here?"

"Stop this! I didn't bring you out here to talk about the past, but of the future."

His eyes were wide, his posture angry. She felt fear emerging for the first time that evening. "Why did you bring me here?"

He stepped in front of her, his hand coming up to cup her cheek once more, not letting go this time, his fingers stroking lightly. She forced herself not to pull away.

"I like you," he said. "I wanted to spend time with you alone. Do I shock you?"

"No."

You scare the fuck out of me.

Her senses were on high alert, from the light breeze

across her skin to the smell of freshly cultivated dirt. She sensed something else, too.

They were being watched, and not just by Jerome in the watchtower. There was someone out there, on the other side of the fence.

Was that possible?

He leaned toward her ever so slightly and she pulled away. His eyes hardened.

"I'm not used to men," she said, the lie coming easily to her lips. "You're right about that."

His demeanor changed immediately. "You are meant for me. You've waited your whole life for my touch. Just one kiss then."

She shouldn't have come out here, shouldn't have allowed herself to be alone with this psycho, and she considered using a few self-defense moves on him to get him to the ground.

And then what? Do you think they'll let you stay on and search for Julianne after you've beat up their leader?

He slipped his hand behind her head, holding her still. The fear that had come alive when they first came out here had her transfixed. David moved in for a kiss.

Something hard hit the compound fence behind them and they jerked apart.

"What the hell was that?" David barked.

Her heartbeat was skipping in her chest.

Definitely not alone.

"I'm sure it was just an animal."

"Jerome! Fire into the woods!"

"What are you doing?" she asked frantically, suddenly worried the guard would hurt the interloper. "There's a fence. We're safe here."

The guard fired five shots in quick succession, the loud popping noise making her cover her ears.

The sound of people running came at them from the direction of the dormitories.

"Jerome, turn off the light," called David.

Cassidy stared into the darkness, wishing she could see who was out there, imagining a dead or frightened man, or beast.

"Brother David, what happened?" asked a man behind her.

Thomas.

"A bear in the distance. We scared it off."

"Thank goodness you were here to take care of it," someone else said.

"God is good. Now back to bed for us all," said David. "There will be no more shooting tonight."

The crowd murmured its thanks and began to leave. Cassidy wanted to go too—as far away from this man as she could get. "I'm going to turn in for the night."

"All right then." He picked up her hand and kissed the back of it. "Until tomorrow."

She swallowed bile. "Until tomorrow."

6

A ustin hit the ground the second he heard the gunshots, his weapon in his hand before his belly hit the dirt, but he didn't fire back.

He didn't need to.

He'd thrown the rock at the fence on impulse as the couple was about to kiss. He should have been too far away to tell for sure, but he could tell by her posture and the way she moved it was Cassidy. The other one looked like David Kelleher—a possibility he could barely even admit to himself right now.

It was the unease he sensed in the way she held herself that had him throwing the rock. She didn't want that man— whoever he was—so close to her.

Or so you think.

Hell, maybe he was wrong, but once his protective instincts were sounding the alarm there wasn't any stopping them.

Hopefully you didn't give your position away, asshole.

Things went bump in the night all the time. A rock hitting a fence could easily be mistaken for an animal of some kind. Shit, they had bears and moose and elk and all sorts of crap up here. This part of Idaho was like a goddamn zoo.

He narrowed his eyes as he watched the people return to their buildings through his night vision goggles, Cassidy and the man included.

He followed her from the other side of the fence, hiding himself far enough into the woods to avoid detection. A half mile away from where she began, she and about half the other women ducked into a long log-cabin.

First things first. He had to get inside.

He took off his goggles and opened his pack, withdrawing the bolt cutters. The fence wasn't electrified, so that would be his easiest route inside.

He crawled slowly to the perimeter of the compound, confident his camouflage clothing would conceal him, and began cutting away at the chain-link fence. He'd selected a dark area illuminated by a single sodium light more than a hundred feet away.

Carefully he cut an eighteen-inch vertical line from the ground to the height of his head, then he moved over three feet and did it again. He was capable of crawling through a smaller opening, but on the return trip he'd have Cassidy with him—hopefully walking on two feet instead of kicking and screaming or unconscious.

If she didn't want to leave, he would knock her out with the drugs in his pack and carry her out of here. He was prepared for any eventuality with smoke bombs and noise grenades that should provide enough cover for him to make it out of here if need be, but he was sure as hell partial to sneaking out quietly with no one in pursuit.

A moving light caught his eye and he pulled his binoculars to his face. A woman was walking outside the dormitory carrying a lantern and a towel. When she reached an outdoor shower and hung the light on a high post, he was finally able to see her face.

Cassidy.

She stepped into the wooden stall and stripped, draping her clothing off a bar on the other side of the wall. From Austin's vantage point on a small hill, he could just see the tops of her breasts before she started the water.

There she was. After so much time, her body was just as perfect as he remembered, and he silently hoped she wasn't sharing it with anyone, much less David Kelleher.

She was one hell of a reporter. With her father's notoriety it had been easy to check up on her after one too many beers over the years. When she started working for the *Post*, he started reading the paper—no matter he lived in Atlanta instead of D.C.

He couldn't help but wonder what lengths she'd go to for a story. Her father said she was here to find Julianne but surely the temptation must be great to research The Community as well. He mentally ticked off another reason she wouldn't want to come with him.

How would she react when she saw him?

Fuck that train of thought.

"Time to get this show on the road," he said to himself, noiselessly slipping through the hole in the fence on his way to collect his ex-girlfriend.

7

Cassidy let the hot water sluice over her tired muscles and closed her eyes, the scent of shampoo like a luxury she'd never before appreciated. She still wasn't ready for bed. That was one thing she certainly hadn't gotten used to. The early-to-bed, early-to-rise mentality held by The Community.

She was a night owl. Always had been. She adored the quiet of the night, the twinkle of the stars, the lack of people around to interrupt her thoughts.

The lack of David trying to stick his tongue down my throat.

Her eyes opened, thousands of stars filling her field of view.

"So beautiful."

She hadn't known what to expect when she came here. David had sent a helicopter for her after she contacted him through their website, saying she was intrigued by the ideals of The Community.

They'd flown in late afternoon and by the time they'd finished with the tour, the sun was setting over the Sawtooth

Mountains and she'd been captivated by the beauty of this place.

David had been far less captivating, but from the moment she was introduced she gushed with enthusiasm for The Community and her own desire to join.

She hadn't been home since. She hadn't let her guard down or truly been herself or relaxed beyond her evening outdoor shower after all the other women had gone to sleep. This was her time, her moment to regroup so she could face another day in this place.

She soaped up her back with the handmade soap they all used here, an herbal scent that clung to her skin long after she dried off. It was intoxicating and thick, and it seemed to symbolize her belonging to the group, as if even her own personal scent had been sacrificed for the communal one.

Julianne had bathed in these waters, had been cloaked in this same smell.

The thought made her want to cry, but over the last few weeks she'd gotten very good at keeping her tears at bay. She had to find Julianne, had to learn the fate of her friend even if Julianne herself was gone. And the longer Cassidy was here, the more convinced she became that her friend was no longer alive.

No. She would know if that was the case.

She certainly wasn't part of this group anymore and she never came home, which meant there was a third option that must be true.

What if I never get home either?

"Stop it," she whispered to herself. But the thought had taken hold in her mind. What if she never left the compound, never saw her parents again, wasn't able to leave this place as easily as she'd arrived?

There was no talk of leaving from anyone in The Community. She hadn't been told she was required to stay here, yet it seemed like a given that she was. Hell, there was no disagreement about which vegetables to eat with dinner, and she couldn't imagine anyone disagreeing with David on such a large scale as to ask to leave this place.

The vow was for life.

The soap slipped between her legs, lathering in her curls. Would he take that too? Would her body belong to The Community as well as her soul?

I'll do whatever it takes to find Julianne. Anything I have to do.

She turned, letting the water cascade down her features and opening her mouth to breathe in the humid air.

A deep male voice spoke very close by. "Don't scream."

Her eyes flew open. The shower wall was nearly the same height as her eyes, but the man was taller than she, his face in full view as his stare locked with hers.

"Austin?" She couldn't believe her eyes. She'd seen his face a hundred times in her dreams, in that half-wakeful state between the day and night when she longed to be held in his arms.

She missed his body most of all, that amazing torso made of solid muscle, the arms that held her tight against his nakedness. She and Austin did best when there were no words. Words only got them in trouble.

Her arms covered her breasts. She stood on her tip toes, her eyes darting around. "What the hell are you doing here?"

"I'm here to help you."

"Help me?"

He nodded. "Your parents sent me to bring you home."

"My parents?" Nothing could be more insane. Her

parents hated Austin. They would do anything to keep him away. "They think I'm in Paris."

"Not anymore, sweetheart. They checked up on you in France and realized you'd never made the trip. It didn't take a lot of snooping to find out where you'd gone, or so I hear. We weren't brought in until after that."

"We?"

"HERO Force. My teammates and me. It stands for Hands-on Engagement and Recognizance Operations. We got separated after a parachute accident. I'm the only one who made it to the ranch."

She scoffed. "Not much of a rescue."

He raised one eyebrow. "I can handle it."

The distant sound of footsteps on gravel had her adrenaline pumping. "Someone's coming. You have to hide."

He crouched down so that he was hidden by the shower wall. Cassidy again put her head beneath the shower spray, listening as the footsteps grew closer and the person rounded the corner not far from the shower.

What would happen if they found Austin here? She thought of her virgin lie to David just now. Surely anyone could look at her and Austin together and see the giant neon sign over their heads that read WE USED TO BE LOVERS.

And damn it if she wasn't getting wet down there already just from him showing up to "save" her. Not that she needed saving, but all that man had to do was be within five feet of her body to get her insides all dewy, warm and aching for a nice, hard fuck.

Stop it.

The door to her shower stall rattled lightly and she realized Austin had moved around opposite their guest, and now wanted to come inside.

"No!" she hissed quietly.

"Beautiful night, isn't it Sister Cassidy?" came another man's voice.

David.

Fuck!

That man didn't know how to take no for an answer. How could she explain she wasn't a virgin sent by God like some kind of third-century Christmas present? "Yes, it is," she said, furiously soaping her body.

What was he doing here? And what would he do if he found Austin? She slid open the bolt and let Austin inside, the stall now incredibly crowded. He'd removed his shirt, his dark chest hair a dangerous shadow in the tight space.

"I've seen you down here late at night, taking showers when the other women are sleeping," David said.

"It's hard for me to get to sleep." Austin was curled in on himself, squatting on an upside-down milk crate in the corner of the shower stall, his head less than a foot from her naked breasts.

David chuckled. "I can relate. I found it impossible to get to sleep this evening, myself." During that sentence he had walked so close to the shower, he must be directly on the other side of the wall. He wasn't as tall as Austin, however, which prevented him from making eye contact with her.

"I kept thinking about you," he said. "Imagining we'd had the opportunity to finish that kiss."

Her face crumpled and she shivered despite the hot water running down her body. She'd never been so disgusted by a man as she was in that moment, and the sudden and surprising presence of Austin by her side was the only sense of safety she possessed.

Her eyes locked with Austin's in the darkness and she knew he could clearly see her fear. Still she said, "I do, too."

"The temptation to be near you is great, Sister Cassidy."

She squeezed her eyes shut. "Perhaps in the morning we can have breakfast together."

"And if I can't wait until morning? If I give in to these feelings you stir inside of me?"

She shook her head, frantic now. "No."

"You're afraid. You know not man. But I can show you things that will make you happy. Make you feel good."

Cassidy dropped her chin to her chest. She couldn't even look at Austin's reaction to that one. "Those things are for a husband and wife."

David laughed. "Indeed they are. And you shall be mine. Now let me inside."

Her hands went to the door, holding it closed despite its lock. "No!" She bit her lip. She caught a glimpse of Austin's face, surprised to see the anger so clearly painted on his features. Aware of his judgment of her. Aware of her own nakedness and the horrible light in which she appeared. "I want it to be special when we are married."

"Then we must marry very quickly, before the temptation overtakes me." David sighed. "I will go home. In the morning we will talk again."

"I would like that."

His footsteps could be heard retreating. When he was gone, Austin spoke. "Turn off the lantern."

She did as he asked, aware of his body coming to its full height beside her. He turned off the water.

"You know not man?"

She sighed. "I lied."

"I remember." He touched her shoulder, the connection sending a bolt of excitement up her arm and down her body, lighting up her senses on the way.

He cursed under his breath before he kissed her, his

mouth finding hers unerringly in the dark. He tasted so familiar, her body instantly remembering what this man could do to her and readying itself for his assault.

Her arms snaked up his naked chest, reveling in the feel of his wet hair and skin. She hadn't imagined this, hadn't blown up the attraction in her mind to some level it never truly attained. This was real, damn it, every bit—and her sexual experiences since him paled meekly in comparison.

She stepped on the milk crate and leaned into him, knowing before he did that he would grab her ass and hold her against his stiffening cock. His tactical fatigues were rough and wet, covered in pockets and belt loops that rubbed the sensitive flesh of her sex.

He was kissing her face, her forehead, her neck, and she imagined he would leave behind bruises as he roughly sucked at her skin.

Then he was trying to pull away, slow down what was happening between them, and she brought his hand up to her breast, moaning when he squeezed it.

He cursed again. "You need to get dressed. We don't have a lot of time."

"No, you need to get undressed. It's easier to fuck you that way." She threw herself back into his arms, kissing him, his arms coming around her once more.

"Jesus, Cass." He ground against her. "I need you to come with me. Please get some clothes on."

She bit his ear. "That isn't really what you want."

"Now, Cassidy! We have to go before someone catches me here."

She leaned back. "What?"

"We need to leave."

"I'm not going anywhere. I need to find—"

"You're looking for your friend. Your parents told me all

about it. But Cassidy, her press credentials were mailed to her editor at the *Washington Post*, along with her necklace. She was discovered. She's gone, sweetie."

She shook her head frantically. "No. That's not possible. I got a ping from her on my satellite phone yesterday."

"A ping?"

"Yeah. It's just a blip, no information, but it shows she tried to contact me."

"It must have been someone else."

"No. She's alive."

"How else would those things have shown up in the mail? They were bloody, Cassidy."

"I don't know, but there must be some rational explanation."

"It's not safe for you here."

"I'm not just going to leave her!"

He crossed his arms. "What's your plan, then? You really going to marry that guy?"

"If I have to do that to find her, then yes."

"Unfuckingbelievable." The disdain in his voice was no different than the disdain in her heart, but she hated that it was directed at her, that he'd so quickly judged her and found her lacking. He grabbed her clothes and handed them to her.

"Will you turn around please?" she asked.

"You're kidding."

"No."

He turned to face the wall and she pulled up her panties and tugged on her clothes, with more than a little regret. "I'm done."

He turned around and met her stare. "You're sure you won't come with me?"

She shook her head. "Positive."

"Then I'm sorry I have to do this."

Before she realized what he was about, he reached around her with arms seemingly made of steel. A sharp sting in her ass cheek made her gasp with surprise. "What are you doing?"

"Rest for a while, sweetheart."

She felt drunk almost immediately, the dizziness in her head suddenly overpowering her consciousness. She didn't understand what was happening, could barely understand what he'd done.

He drugged me. He injected me with something.

"Bastard," was all she got out.

Her eyelids were too heavy for her to keep her eyes open and she fought for balance. Were those his hands on her upper arms? She was going to fall. That was her last thought before she completely lost consciousness.

ustin heated his MRE with a chemical pack. It was too risky to light a fire just in case anyone realized Cassidy had left the compound and came searching for her tonight. With her added weight he hadn't been able to get as far as he would've liked, only a mile and a half, maybe two.

He set up his tent on the top of a small hill and snuggled her inside it. It had already been more than two hours since he knocked her out with the injection and he wondered if she was still unconscious or simply asleep.

She's going to wake up around about the time I cozy up next to her.

And she was bound to be mighty pissed this time around, not like she was in the shower.

Just the thought of it had his cock leaping to life. Five hot seconds in her presence and he'd all but fucked her against the shower wall. She would have let him, too. After all this time, she would have let him come right back inside her body like they'd never even stopped being lovers.

That was a heady truth to swallow.

He pulled out cornbread and broke off a piece, unseeing.
What did you expect?

He had to think about that one for a minute, his mind
going back over their last meeting.

Disdain.

She'd seemed so much better than him that day, as if
she'd slipped on a pair of shoes that made her taller than
anyone else could possibly be. They weren't right for each
other. They were just too different.

He knew what that meant. He wasn't good enough for
her, would never run in the same circles as her wealthy and
politically connected family. He was a scrub from Brooklyn,
the way he talked not suitable for certain functions.

Hell, it would be better if she'd been like that now
instead of throwing her naked self around him like a pretzel,
all but begging him to have sex with her.

He could hear David Kelleher's voice in his head, hear
the desire in it as he talked about pleasuring Cassidy with
his body. About marrying her. That bastard didn't know
how close he'd come to a punch to the throat and a knot in
his balls, but Cassidy had allowed him to talk to her
that way.

No. *She'd encouraged it.*

And that turned his blood into some toxic mix of testos-
terone and adrenaline so that he couldn't decide what to do
first—kick David's ass or fuck hers.

*Keep your dick in your pants and your head in the game,
asshole.*

The sound of nylon rubbing against nylon alerted him
to her wakefulness. It was a cloudless night, with enough
moonlight to illuminate their small camp reasonably well.

"Cassidy?"

The noises stopped. "You knocked me out."

"I had to get you out of there without you making a scene."

More rustling, then the sound of the tent zipper unzipping. "You took me away from The Community?"

"Yep."

She climbed out of the small tent and stood, looking around at the woods that surrounded them, the peaks of her nipples standing out against the fabric of her shirt. "You had no right to do that! I wanted to be there. You had no right to take me away!"

He shrugged. "It's my job. I told you, your parents are worried about you and they sent me to find you and bring you home."

"And I'm worried about Julianne and trying to find *her* and bring her home."

"She's dead, Cassidy."

She put her hands on her hips. When she spoke, her voice was trembling. "You've got it wrong. She's alive and David is the key to her disappearance. I've been trying to get close to him so I can find out what happened. He was going to have Lucas give me a tour of the ranch tomorrow."

He narrowed his eyes. "If you're right and she's alive, I'll come back here myself and get her just as soon as I bring you home."

Cassidy waved her arm in the air. "Why not go back right now? We can't be far away, and I left my satellite phone, my notes, everything. She needs our help, Austin."

"I need to make sure you're safe. I don't want you back there with that crazy bastard."

She crossed to him and pushed his chest. "You don't get to tell me what to do."

"Your parents hired HERO Force to find you and bring you back, and that's what I'm doing."

"What kind of hero leaves a woman to die? She's pregnant. Did you know that?" She covered her mouth with her hand.

"She's already gone. I'm sorry for your friend, Cassidy, and I'm sorry for her baby, I really am. But she's dead and putting yourself in harm's way isn't going to bring her back." He picked up the MRE and held it out toward her. "Eat something. You need your strength."

She knocked the food to the ground. "If you won't take me back, I'll go on my own."

He all but growled with frustration. "Be my guest. We're a couple of miles away. I figure even if you head out in the right direction, you don't have any kind of protection against bears or coyotes, do you? Because they make quick work of a cute little meal like you."

She looked around, seeming to consider each direction as if looking for a star in the sky to guide her. Her eyes slowly came back to his. "Damn it, Austin. Don't do this."

He looked away. "I'm not doing anything. You lied to your family and you've been hiding at some kind of cult for weeks now. Your boss didn't want you there and your colleague has already lost her life. It's right for me to bring you home. If you can't see that, then I guess you'll just have to cry to Daddy when we get there."

She slapped his face. He saw it coming—could have stopped it even—but he did not. In the silence that followed, they eyed each other angrily. She was the first to speak. "I don't go crying to my Daddy anymore. And if you had an ounce of sense in that thick head of yours, you'd see I'm trying to do the right thing for once in my life."

She turned away. "I'm going to go back to sleep and

tomorrow morning I'm heading back to The Community."
She crawled into the tent, nylon rustling until it was once
again quiet in the forest.

9

Jax paced the length of the operations room, Noah on a computer and Logan in a wheelchair, his leg outstretched and covered in a camouflage patterned cast.

His femur had been snapped in two when he hit the ground. He would have been dead if Noah hadn't grabbed him and held onto him until they hit the tree line, his parachute failing completely. The accident threw them off course by nearly a half mile.

It was Noah who got Logan out of those woods and back to safety, Noah's medical skills that kept Logan from bleeding out and dying. It would be six months or more before Logan's leg healed completely.

Cowboy leaned over Noah's shoulder, chanting, "Come on you motherfucker. Where the hell are you?"

Austin's geolocation beacon was malfunctioning, only broadcasting a signal intermittently. The last time they connected, it showed he was inside Longwood Ranch.

"I can't believe he went in there alone," said Jax. "It was careless. No—stupid." He ran a hand through his hair.

Cowboy moved to a chair and sat in it backwards. "It was the timetable. He knew if he didn't try for the compound, he wouldn't have time to get back here and regroup."

"Doesn't do him or the senator's daughter a shit ton of good if he's dead," said Jax.

"He just might make it," said Cowboy.

"If he does, I'm going to fire his ass. I don't need a renegade I can't trust to make good decisions running loose out there."

"He knows her," said Noah. All heads turned in his direction.

"Come again?" asked Cowboy.

"When we were on the tarmac waiting to takeoff, he told me she'd once been his girlfriend. He didn't tell you guys that?"

Jax put his hands on his hips. "Fuck." He shook his head. "Double fuck. Why didn't somebody share this little tidbit of information with me? He had no business going up in that plane in the first place."

Cowboy shrugged. "We knew the Lanes were personal friends of his. That's why they came to us."

"Being friends with an old man and screwing that man's daughter on an ongoing basis is not the same thing," said Jax. "Do any of you think he went into The Community alone because he felt a sense of duty to the senator and his wife?"

No one answered.

"That's right," said Jax. "He went in there because he's making decisions with his dick instead of his goddamn brain. We need to mobilize. Get the fuck back out there in case he needs our help."

"Noah, you and I go wheels up within the hour. You

ready to jump out of a plane again after what happened the last time?" asked Cowboy.

"Absofuckinlutely."

"Good. No fancy moves this time." Cowboy winked.

"Happy to oblige."

10

Cassidy was so frustrated she wanted to scream. Austin Dixon—what a blast from the past that name was—was screwing up the most important thing she'd ever done in her life. Julianne was alive. She knew it. She had to convince him to go back.

She thought of her parents and frowned. She never intended for them to find out. Since when were they in the habit of checking up on her? Since her father entered politics when she was ten years old, they'd seemingly lost interest in their only daughter. She knew they loved her, sure. But worry for her? Wonder where she was or doubt what she had told them? Never.

She was the responsible daughter of a responsible man. A reporter for one of the most well respected newspapers in the country. She was not a child and she didn't appreciate being treated like one.

Especially by a man I just threw myself at, naked.

That was the rub. Despite what he'd done she was still painfully attracted to him, like her twenty-year-old self had taken over her thirty-year-old body. She was a walking hormone—angry as hell and hornier than she had any right to be.

Fuck him.

Yeah, you'd like that, wouldn't you?

Breaking up with Austin had been incredibly difficult, and it had forever changed the relationship between her and her parents. He wasn't suitable marriage material, said her mother—a dozen photos from a tabloid photographer in a neat pile between them. And what will people *say*?

Her father was up for re-election. The photographer was considerate enough to sell the photos to the senator instead of sullying his daughter's good name with the pictures of her making love to a sailor on a speedboat in the middle of the Chesapeake Bay.

They'd taken something beautiful and made it ugly, then they used it to blackmail her parents and control her actions.

When Austin had shown up outside her shower, something inside her snapped. Every pent-up emotion she'd been holding inside since he left her life came crashing into her present like a dam breaking loose. She'd shown Austin her lust, but what she'd really been feeling was the memory of overwhelming love.

Careful, Cassidy.

He didn't love her. Never had. Hell, he didn't even respect her enough to listen to her wishes and help her save Julianne. Her mouth turned down in a hard frown. God, was it possible he was right? Could Julianne and the baby be dead?

All the sadness she'd kept at bay rose up and overwhelmed her, every tear she'd forced to stay inside during her time with The Community now flowing out of her eyes and down her cheeks.

She must have cried herself to sleep, because the next thing she knew the zipper on the tent was opening and Austin was climbing in. "You've got to be kidding. Isn't there another tent?" she asked, exasperated.

"Yep. It's in Logan's pack."

"Let me guess. Logan's one of the guys you got separated from."

"That's right. Scoot over. I'll keep you warm."

That did hold a certain appeal. The tent wasn't cold exactly, but it was a far cry from warm. She moved over but barely managed to make room for him anyway.

Perfect.

Just what I need right now—another close encounter with Austin.

Her head ached dully from her crying and she didn't feel equipped to defend herself against her feelings for this man right now. When he settled and opened his arm for her to cuddle against his side as he'd done so many times before, she froze.

"Come here," he said so casually, she simply complied, her head resting on his t-shirt-covered chest and his arm sliding down her back. He stroked her gently, just as he used to do, and Cassidy was filled with emotion.

Better not examine that too closely.

Besides, she needed to be worrying about Julianne right now, not her unresolved feelings for Austin.

"Do you really think she's dead?"

"Yes. I'm sorry, Cass."

"She's my best friend. We started at the *Post* together right out of college. We got all the shit assignments together, and we had to prove to our editor we could handle more, each of us on our own stories but seeming to mirror each other's journey, you know?"

Austin kissed the top of her head and let her cry. He continued to stroke her back. It felt so good to be in his arms, so familiar and safe, and she reminded herself how angry she was with him for making her leave the compound.

It would be so easy to lift her head and kiss him, no one nearby to interrupt them this time. But she had to be smart. They couldn't be far away from the ranch. Austin was strong, but she didn't imagine he was strong enough to carry her forever. It wasn't too late to convince him to go back. Sleeping with him and tapping into the feelings they'd once shared could only help her get her way, not hurt her chances.

Except the feelings had been hers, their relationship one-sided in that regard. Austin had been all-in for the sex, but she was the only one who'd fallen in love, and she knew if she slept with him now it would bring up all the old feelings. She would feel just as tethered to him emotionally as she had been all those years before.

No. I'm stronger now.

I'm not the same person I was then.

Maybe she could survive a tryst with him and keep right on going instead of crashing her love life into a tree. Her leg curled higher on his and he moaned softly.

Nobody to interrupt them.

Nothing to stop them.

If she responded to him, they would make love.

And my heart will be broken all over again.

No. He wasn't the man for her. She knew that and couldn't let herself forget. It wasn't just the way he talked like a New York City cabby, or that he'd stand out at political functions like a sore thumb. The problem was so much deeper than that.

He could never be happy with a woman like her.

Austin wanted a wife who came with a crockpot in tow, not an investigative reporter who loved her job more than breathing and lived on takeout and microwave quesadillas. He wanted babies and homemade desserts. The one time he brought her to meet his family, his mother had all but chased her out of the house with a wooden spoon before locking the door and making the sign of the cross.

She was nice to you. You're imagining things.

But she knew she was not. Mama Dixon could see what Cassidy herself was trying so hard to turn a blind eye to. She and Austin were not well-suited out of the sack.

But oh, when they were in it...

She curled her fingers before stroking her fingers down his abdomen. She longed to see if he was hard, but her embarrassment would be complete if he was not. She imagined what he would feel like inside of her again, the hard ground beneath her hips as they came together.

"I'm still mad at you," she said.

"I know." He lifted his head and kissed her, curling onto his side. Blood rushed between her legs, engorging her sex, making her even more desperate for his touch.

She pushed him backward and straddled his hips, glorying in the feel of his rock hard erection against her entrance. "I still want to go back. This doesn't mean we're done fighting."

He lifted her shirt and she yanked it over her head. "I know."

He pulled her down to him, taking a nipple in his mouth and lavishing it with his tongue before sucking her deeply. She bucked against his cock and offered him the other breast.

"Tell me you have a condom in these fucking Inspector Gadget pants somewhere."

He chuckled, reaching down to a small pocket near his right knee and withdrawing a foil packet. "Survivalist training 101."

She moved down his body until his belt buckle was in front of her face and unbuckled it, unzipping his pants and releasing his cock straight into her mouth. He cried out as she sucked him, deep throating him like she knew he liked.

"Jesus, Cassy, stop or I'm going to come."

She lifted her head and he flipped her over with one strong movement, putting her firmly beneath him. She quickly pulled her panties down and his fingers nestled in the hair between her legs until he found her clitoris, gently stroking with one finger while another toyed with her entrance.

"Oh my God, I've forgotten how good this feels," she whispered with an urgency that demanded he continue.

"Sex in general, or sex with me?"

He was torturing her, making her reveal her secrets under duress, and she fought against the admission.

"Answer me, Cassidy."

She ground out on a moan. "You. The best sex was always with you."

He sheathed himself and climbed on top of her, filling her completely with one hard thrust. Just like that she was flying, her body anchored to the ground by his fierce love-making and her soul soaring high above.

Then she was back in her body, digging her nails into the bunched muscles of his back, inhaling the musk of his overheated skin deep into her lungs. The unforgiving earth increased the power of his wild thrusts, pinioning her between his driving body and the bracing ground, and her climax ripped through her like wildfire on a dry summer field.

Then Austin was exploding too, his body emptying itself as he convulsed in the final throes of passion. They stayed together, intimately connected as her breathing slowed, Cassidy staring her feelings for Austin straight in the eye, unflinching.

I love him.

I never stopped loving him. Wishing he'd come back.

"Me too," he whispered.

She stopped breathing. "What?"

"Sex was always best with you—for me, too."

Disappointment was sharp and thorny. She pushed at him lightly and he moved off her, turning his back to deal with the condom before moving beside her once more.

She tried to settle anywhere but on top of him, but there simply wasn't room in the tent. She gave up, frustrated, and leaned back next to him.

"What if I'm right, Austin? What if she's alive?"

He sighed heavily. "I can't take that chance. By morning they'll know you're gone, if they don't already. They're not going to let me in there with you to keep you safe. They're going to harass you with questions, at the very least. God only knows what Kelleher will do to you if he doesn't trust you anymore. It's too late, Cassidy. It isn't safe. I'm sorry."

"Last night in the shower before you came along, I was thinking of her and wondering if she was still alive. She's not in the compound. She's not out of it and back to her old life. She's somewhere in between, like some sort of invisible limbo, and I'm the only one who knows she's there or is doing anything about it. I have to find her."

"No. We need to get moving. It will be light soon."

"I'm not going with you. So I hope you have lots of whatever the hell you stuck in my ass cheek last night, because you're going to need it if you think I'm going one more step away from my friend who needs me."

"We can do this the hard way or the easy way. That's up to you."

"I'll press charges when we get back. Kidnapping. I don't think the military would look too favorably on that."

"Probably not, but I'm retired. I work for HERO Force now, remember? And they just want you back. They don't give a shit how I do it."

She crossed her arms over her chest. "I told you, I'm not coming with you."

"Suit yourself. Just remember it gets down below freezing here at night, and you won't have a tent or my body to keep you warm. You don't know which way to go to get back to the compound. And if you get lost in these woods, there's no one to search for you, much less find you. But by all means, if you want to go back to that wacko in the woods, be my guest."

She rolled over, presenting him with her back. She would wake up before him, find his compass and leave before he had any idea she was gone.

11

Austin rolled over, half awake. It took him a second to remember where he was — the tent, the woods, Cassidy. His eyes popped open.

He was alone in the tent, the early light of morning shining all around him.

"Cassidy?"

She didn't answer. He remembered the feel of her beneath him, coming apart as she climaxed. He shook his head. He never would've thought in a million years he'd be with her again. Never could have dreamed how good it would be.

It changed things. He wasn't willing to have her walk out of his life again, at least not without a fight.

Are you sure you want to do that?

He remembered all too well that she hadn't fought for him last time. On the contrary, she'd been more than happy to let him go. He told himself it was a long time ago, and he told himself he was dreaming. Just because he wanted Cassidy did not mean Cassidy wanted to be with him.

Never going to find out if I don't give it a try.

And sex like they'd had last night demanded he give it a try.

Feeling determined, he climbed out of the tent ready to face her. No doubt, she would start the day as she had ended the last — lobbying to return to The Community. That woman was about a stubborn as they came.

He stood to his full height, Cassidy nowhere in sight. He spun in a slow circle calling her name.

She wasn't here.

"Oh, fuck." He climbed back into the tent, a sense of foreboding telling him what he would find before he checked the pockets on his tactical pants. Sure enough, his compass was gone, and he'd bet money she'd found the map of the mountain in his pack and taken that, too.

He cursed a blue streak as he dressed and quickly took down the tent, stuffing it in his pack. God only knew how long she'd been gone and if he be able to find her at all.

He'd been stupid not to take her at her word. She told him what she was going to do, he just didn't think she would do it. He made a mental note not to underestimate Cassidy Lane in the future.

He moved quickly, jogging in the direction of the compound. She left him his watch, all his weapons, and most concerning, his canteen. From the time he could roughly estimate the position of the sun and hence direction, but she wasn't prepared for her journey at all.

He moved faster, chanting to the rhythm of his footfalls. "Please let me find her. Please let me find her."

A high-pitched scream echoed through the forest.

Her name was ripped from his vocal cords. "Cassidy?" She was in trouble—hurt or scared, or God knows what— and he had to get to her quickly. He flew through the trees, waving and bobbing around obstacles, his ears trained on the particular frequency of her voice as he yelled for her.

Another scream as he shifted direction, cresting a small hill before she came into view. In her bright colored clothing she was easy to spot, and it took him a moment to realize the problem. A big brown bear stood just twenty feet from her location, clearly staring her down.

"Don't move!" he yelled.

The bear turned his head to stare at Austin, the distinct rumbling of its low growl carrying across the forest floor.

"Don't move," he called again. "If he comes any closer, drop to the ground and play dead. Whatever you do, don't run."

The bear growled more loudly and got up on his hind legs, looking from Austin to Cassidy and back again. Austin wanted to go to her and put himself between her and harm's way, but any forward movement would encourage the bear to attack.

He sat down on the ground and reached into his pack, withdrawing his firearm and readying the weapon. It was a larger caliber then he normally carried, but seeing the size of the bear, he wondered if it would be enough to take the animal down if need be.

They stayed frozen like that, moments seeming to last for hours, Cassidy unmoving, and the bear growling, and Austin with his sights lined up on the beast.

The moment the bear moved toward her, she was on the ground and Austin emptied his semiautomatic weapon into the animal.

Then he was running toward her, the bear dead and Cassidy screaming until she was wrapped tightly in his arms. "What are you doing out here by yourself?" he snapped. "You could've been killed, dammit."

"I didn't know. I didn't realize…"

"I told you. I tried to keep you safe."

"I'm sorry." She was sobbing now, her breath coming in great heaving gasps. "But I had to get to Julianne."

He grabbed her by the shoulders, wanting to shake her for the danger she had put herself in. "She's gone, Cassidy! You nearly got yourself killed for a dead woman."

Her eyes darkened and she pulled away from his grasp. "I'll do it again, too." She stood and walked away from him.

"Cassidy, stop!"

She spun around. "I won't stop. Julianne is alive and I'm going back for her, and if that gets me killed then so be it."

He grabbed his forehead. She was crazy, determined to have her way no matter the cost.

Crazy, or else she's right.

"Wait."

She stopped walking and turned to face him, her expression full of emotion.

"You win," he said. He walked toward her. "If you are so convinced you're willing to risk your own life after almost just losing it, then I will go with you."

Her eyebrows shot up. "You will? Do you believe she's alive?"

He didn't, not for a second, and the truth should have scared him to the core. He touched her cheek. "I believe I would follow you off the edge of a cliff if you asked me to."

"You think she's dead, but you're willing to go anyway?"

"Yep. That about sums it up. Can I have my map and compass?"

She dug them out of her pockets and he checked their location. "We've only got another eight or nine hundred feet to go."

She started off in the same direction she'd been heading.

"Not that way." He pointed in a completely different direction. "That way."

"Oh. I guess it's a good thing you're here." She chuckled. "I should have stayed in Girl Scouts."

"Why didn't you?"

She walked past him. "They were a bunch of bitches."

He laughed, realizing again how much he liked her. He was heading toward a crazy man just to make her happy.

You are in a world of shit, Austin.

12

The sound of Austin retching had Cassidy's sympathies on a string. She couldn't see him in the darkness, could only make out a boulder near the path he had taken to be sick. "Are you okay?" she called.

A dark laugh made its way to her ears through the forest. "I think the poison is working."

"Are you going to be able to walk?"

He didn't answer her immediately, and she feared they'd done this all for nothing. She swallowed hard against the dryness in her throat. "Austin?"

A dark shadow emerged near the boulder, slowly straightening to his full height. "I'm okay." He walked toward her, his gait unsteady. "I think it's a good thing we waited until we were close to the compound before I took it."

She could see his face now, glistening in the light from the clouded moon. She reached up and touched his forehead, finding it cold and wet. "I'm sorry you have to do this," she whispered.

"I'm fine. Let's roll."

They walked together the last quarter-mile, the lights from the compound coming into view in the distance. "Hang on a sec," he said, doubling over and vomiting beside his feet.

The poison nettle he'd ingested was having the desired effect. He seemed terribly ill, sick enough that the others in The Community would want to take care of him, or so she hoped. She couldn't bear to think of what might happen if they turned him away. She'd have to go back in there herself and face David alone.

A shiver made her shoulders shimmy at the thought. David was bound to be angry with her for leaving, at the very least. Sometimes he was so kind, so forgiving. But others he was ruthless, his anger seeming to rise up from nowhere like a snake on the attack. If he was upset with her, she would know it. And God only knew what would happen then.

Maybe that's what happened to Julianne.

Maybe she made David angry. Maybe she'd even tried to escape, as Cassidy herself had.

You didn't try to escape. Austin took you.

That was true, but she had no intention of telling David about Austin's role in her disappearance. She would claim she had left of her own free will, using a pair of bolt cutters from the shed to cut through the chain-link fence. She and Austin had stayed up deep into the night planning even the minute details of their return to The Community. She knew what she had to say, she was just terrified of her believability when she said it.

She'd never been a very good liar.

Austin righted himself beside her and walked again, the smell of vomit putrid on the cold night air.

"You're sure that isn't going to kill you?"

"Nope. Didn't take enough. Just two leaves. I should be sick as a dog for the next two or three hours, and okay after that. Assuming I survive that long, of course."

She hit his arm playfully. "That's not funny." She could see the guard tower in the distance, and forced her feet to continue forward.

"You know what you need to say to them, right?"

She nodded. "This man needs help. I ran away because I was afraid of my feelings for David. I found you and you helped me, but I could tell right away you weren't doing well. You convinced me to come back here, but in the meantime your health deteriorated to the point where you became like you are now — high fever, severe nausea, shakes and chills."

"Don't forget the headaches and the seizures."

"You didn't say anything about seizures."

"I didn't want to scare you. They're coming."

"Geez, Austin. What have you done to yourself?"

"I didn't hear you coming up with any great ideas."

They'd brainstormed for hours trying to find a way to get him into the compound strong and well, but in every scenario they imagined he'd be seen as a threat. This way, at least, he was bound to illicit their sympathy, even if that meant he'd be unable to help Cassidy while he was ill.

The effects of the poison nettle were intense but brief. All Cassidy had to do was keep herself safe during that time, which would be easy as long as David believed she was sincere about wanting to be part of The Community again, and part of his life in particular.

Beside her, Austin fell to the ground like a marionette whose puppeteer had dropped its strings. She gasped and knelt down beside him, suddenly certain he'd ingested too much of the poison. "Are you okay?" She touched his over-heated face.

He was doubled over in pain, his knees drawn up to his chest, but he smiled sideways. "Looks like you're going to have to walk the last hundred feet without me, sweetheart."

Genuinely worried now, she stood and started to jog. "I'll get help."

"Wait!" he called, making her turn around. "Walk. You don't want to scare the guy with a gun."

"Jerome."

"Whatever."

"Right. Okay." She forced her legs to walk at a normal pace, feeling stupid for her unthinking run. Austin was so calm and collected in the face of their deception, while she was half-panicked and the other half downright terrified.

The razor wire atop the fence was glinting like some macabre decoration.

You can do this. Austin needs you. Julianne needs you.

She was twenty feet from the gate. She yelled, "Help me, please!" but it came out as little more than a hoarse whisper. She raised her hands above her head in the classic sign for surrender, just like Austin had told her to do. She cleared her throat. "Help me, please!"

This time there was movement from the guard tower closest to her. A light whipped around the perimeter of the property, landing on her with a blinding beam, even in the waning daylight. She forced air into her lungs. "Please, help!"

She made her way to the fence and gripped the thick metal wires in her hands. She could hear footsteps, people running toward her, and another sound as well — familiar from TV and movies.

The metallic sounds of weapons being readied.

Oh, God, I'm going to die.

So is Austin.

She suddenly felt so responsible for that man. If it weren't for her, he wouldn't be here at all. What had she done by coming here in search of Julianne? She thought of her parents, so worried that they sent people to look for her. They must be so afraid for their only daughter. She should have known better. Told them the truth, or something besides just leaving without a word, assuming they wouldn't check up on her.

"I'm sorry," she whispered under her breath. She swiped at her cheek, surprised to realize she was crying. Three men jogged toward her, the one in the middle taller and lankier than the others. David.

"It's me, Cassidy."

There was a hitch in his walk when she identified herself. Then he was in front of her and she was unable to read his features, everyone speaking at once in chaotic conversation through the fence. She hoped she looked like a traumatized and very sorry. "You have to help us, David."

"Us?"

She gestured behind her to where Austin lay on the forest floor. "There's a man. He saved me. He brought me back to you. But he's sick, and I don't know how to help him."

David snapped his fingers. "Let them in."

The men beside him moved to the gate and she let her hand graze the thirty feet of fence that separated her from The Community. David walked beside her even as the others filed out, searching for Austin with bright lights, weapons drawn.

"Don't hurt him!" she yelled.

She could feel the emotion coming from David. Was it

anger? Fury? Or something else? She wondered what awaited her back inside. Then he took her in his arms, holding her tightly against his bony ribs, and she struggled to relax in his arms.

"I thought I'd lost you, Cassidy."

He'd never called her by her first name without the term sister, and the difference could only signify a change in a relationship.

"I'm sorry. I was scared."

He pulled her back from him, holding her at arm's length. "Did he hurt you?"

She shook her head. "No. It wasn't like that. He helped me. Without him I probably wouldn't have made it through the night." She looked at the others, clearly listening to the conversation. Brother Thomas glaring at her like the traitor she knew she was. "I was so stupid."

David followed her stare. "Leave us, Brother Thomas. Tend to the man. We owe him a great debt for bringing Sister Cassidy home."

"Where would you like us to put him?" asked Thomas.

Cassidy put her hand lightly on David's shoulder. "Someplace I can help take care of him."

"As you wish." He raised his voice to be heard by the men. "Take him to my residence. Cassidy, too."

13
_____

Cassidy dipped her washcloth into a bowl of ice water, wringing it out before folding it and placing it back atop Austin's forehead. He had a fever of a hundred and four, his skin incredibly hot to the touch, and he hadn't regained consciousness in the three hours he'd been here.

What if he dies?

Maybe he ate too much of the nettle or confused it for another, more toxic plant.

"You have to get better," she whispered, letting her finger trail down the side of his face. "I can't do this without you."

A voice from behind made her stiffen. "You seem very attached to this man." It was David. She'd been waiting for him to come, but when he failed to materialize she began to relax, thinking he wouldn't demand an explanation for her flight tonight.

She'd been wrong.

She straightened her spine. "He saved my life. It was foolish of me to go out alone on the mountain. I'd be dead if he hadn't appeared and helped me."

He sat down across from her, light from a single candle on Austin's bedside illuminating half his face, leaving the other in shadow. "Why did you leave?"

The smell of alcohol reached her nose, something spicy and sweet. Her toes curled in her shoes. "I was afraid."

"Of The Community?"

She reluctantly met his eyes. "Of you."

"I scared you." He hung his head. "It is part of God's plan that man should be with woman, Sister Cassidy. I didn't mean to scare you."

Neither of them said anything for a few moments.

"How is our patient doing?" he asked.

"Not well. His fever is very high and he hasn't regained consciousness."

"He has the best nurse available, I'm sure." David stood, softly touching her shoulder as he passed, making her flinch. "What's his name?"

"Austin."

"How did he come to be on the mountain?"

"I'm not sure. You'd have to ask him that."

"If he doesn't die tonight, I will." David walked away.

ustin's eyes slowly opened, already searching for Cassidy. He no longer felt like he was dying, so that was an improvement. She sat on the edge of his bed and smiled. He could get used to waking up to her beautiful face especially when she was looking at him like she was right now. "You look better," she said.

"I feel better. Where's David?"

"He went to say morning prayers with The Community."

He lowered his voice. "Did he believe you?"

"I think so, at least for now. But I think he was upset I brought you here. Brother Lucas is coming soon to take me on a tour of the ranch."

"I'm coming too."

"You weren't exactly invited."

"We're in this together. You need to find your friend and I need to bring you back home safely to your mom and pops. We stay together."

"Fine. You weasel yourself an invitation and you're welcome to come. The way David looked at you, I don't think he'll take too kindly to me asking you to join Lucas and me."

"No problem." He swung his legs off the side of the bed, clenching his teeth at the wave of dizziness that followed.

She rushed to his side. "You're still dealing with the toxicity of the nettle. Your thick skull isn't going to get your body through this one."

He rubbed his forehead. "How long have I been out?"

"Five hours."

"Damn it. That's longer than anticipated. Did you find your satellite phone?"

"No. It's not where I left it. The rest of my things are there so I'm sure it was taken."

"Any other problems?" He stood and the room spun, knocking him backwards onto the bed.

"Nope. I just stayed here with you and played nursemaid."

He raised his eyebrows suggestively. "We'll have to try that again sometime when we're out of this place."

"Oh yeah? Maybe with a little nurse's outfit and a hat?"

"And a stethoscope. Nothing turns me on like a stethoscope."

She laughed and looked at her hands. "Thank you for doing this for me."

"You're welcome. But I'm not doing it for free."

"No?"

"I'm going to call in the debt when we get out of this place. I figure you owe me another chance."

"What kind of chance?"

The bedroom door opened, framing David, who looked from Austin to Cassidy and back again. His eyes narrowed almost imperceptibly. "You seem to have made a speedy recovery."

"I'm feeling much better. He held out his hand and introduced himself.

"I hear I owe you my thanks for helping bring Sister Cassidy back to us," said David.

Austin smiled. "She was just telling me she's going on a tour this morning. I'd love to take a look around this beautiful ranch of yours. Mind if I go with her?"

David nodded. "Of course. And then you'll join us for a fine hearty meal before you head on your way. Lucas will be ready momentarily. He'll meet you downstairs."

"Great, I appreciate that very much."

David left the room and Austin turned to Cassidy. "A fine hearty meal before I head on my way. And don't let the door hit you in the ass on your way out."

She stood and crossed to him. "What kind of chance, Austin?"

If they were anywhere but here, he'd answer her with a kiss, maybe more. "For you and me. To see if this can work for real."

The kiss would have been easier. She was staring into his eyes, her expression unreadable, and he was back in her parents' house listening to her tell him all the reasons it wouldn't work.

He had to show her right then that she was wrong, remind her how good they were together. He closed the distance between them, slipped his hand behind her neck to hold her in place and kissed her.

She jerked away from him, her cheeks flushed. "He could walk back in at any moment."

He stared at her lips, red from his touch. "You should answer me now, then."

"We can talk about it when we get out of here."

"Why not talk about it now?"

"Austin, what we have together is incredible. But all the reasons it didn't work the first time are still there."

He frowned. "It didn't work the first time because you thought you were too good for me."

"That isn't true."

"Hell yes, it's true. You and your Mommy and Daddy all agreed. I was okay for a little summer fun, but that's where it needed to stay."

"You don't know what you're talking about."

"I was there, remember? I got to be on the receiving end of your goodbye speech. Let's not pretend now that's not how it happened."

Two spots of color appeared on her cheeks. "As I remember it, you thought I was something special in the sack, as long as I didn't expect anything from you outside of it."

"What's that supposed to mean?"

"Exactly what I said. You wanted to fuck me as long as I didn't actually have feelings for you."

Whoa. What the hell were they talking about here?

Cassidy was acting like the injured party, as if she'd wanted more from the relationship than he'd been ready to give. He tried to think back to who he was then, try to remember what it was he had wanted, but time had distorted reality too much for him to answer that question.

All that mattered now was how she felt today.

"Did you have feelings for me?"

She took a step backwards. "It doesn't matter. That's not the point. The point is you never wanted a real relationship from me, so you don't get to say it was my fault we didn't have one."

"You're the one who broke it off."

"Yes. I was." She put her hands on her hips. "We should go downstairs. Lucas will be waiting for us."

"This is David's house, right?"

She nodded.

"I'm going to look around for a way to contact HERO Force. There must be a phone line or a computer or something. Maybe I'll find your satellite phone."

"I'll stay here in case someone comes. His office is right across the hall."

Austin was much less sturdy on his feet than he expected, and he leaned heavily on the wall when he walked. David's office had an ancient computer, but he couldn't get it to turn on and from the dust on top of it, it could have been sitting here untouched for years.

He went through the desk drawers, hitting pay dirt in the fourth one he tried. A satellite phone, likely Cassidy's. It was even charged up and he dialed the number for HERO Force from memory, unable to remember the cell numbers for the individual men.

"Give me Leo Wilson, quick. It's Austin Dixon."

While he waited to be connected he noticed a large street-level map of Seattle on the wall, about twenty red tacks marking different locations. He stood and leaned in more closely.

The Space Needle.

Pike Place Market.

The Great Wheel and the Art Museum.

"What the fuck?" he whispered. These locations were some of the biggest tourist attractions in the state.

Locations crowded with people.

He got Cowboy's voicemail and he cursed the idiot switchboard operator. "I'm all right. I found Cassidy. She insisted on going back to find Julianne; Cassidy doesn't believe she's dead like the senator said. I found a map of Seattle, Washington with about a dozen major locations highlighted. He's either planning a terrorist attack or the vacation of a lifetime. Send reinforcements."

15

Cassidy sat in the front seat of the truck with Lucas, Austin in the back. The ranch was far larger than she suspected, even after David told her it was over four thousand acres. It was something that had to be seen to be believed.

She was distracted, and while she was looking for anywhere Julianne could possibly be hidden, her mind kept replaying her conversation with Austin.

He wanted a second chance with her. She bit her lip. The first one had knocked her heart around but good. That man had felt like home to her the first night in his bed, and her feelings for him had only grown in the weeks they spent together.

It wasn't rational. She knew that. She hadn't known him long enough to truly fall in love, but the feeling was as real as any she'd had before or since. Which was to say she'd never felt it before — nor felt it after.

There were men in her life. Good men who looked like decent matches on paper. They fit into her world like they were to the manner born, perfectly casted for the role of boyfriend, lover, husband. Yet each one of them had chafed at her soul, only serving to remind her of the man she had lost and the feelings she was incapable of recreating.

I was okay for a little summer fun, but that's where it needed to stay.

His earlier words mocked her. He seemed to think she'd been using him for sex and hell, maybe she had. But Austin Dixon had broken her heart, no matter her initial intentions.

"Pretty impressive, huh?" asked Lucas.

"Definitely," said Cassidy. There were fields upon fields, most lying fallow, unused. "David's parents must have had quite a large business."

"They did, though not by today's commercial farm standards. They were potato growers. It would be hard for a farm this size to sustain itself on potatoes alone these days."

"How did they get their crops to market?" asked Austin. "This place is pretty isolated."

Lucas nodded. "Now it is, but it didn't used to be. There was a dirt road that wound all the way up here from town and the interstate, back in the day. Years of disuse and it all went wild."

"Wasn't it a public road?" asked Austin.

"Oh, no. The Kellehers owned all that back then, all the way down to the highway. When David's parents passed on, he let it all go."

"It seems odd he would choose to be more isolated," said Cassidy.

Lucas chuckled. "If that seems odd, then you don't know David near as well as you think. The farther away he can get from traditional society, the better. That's what makes The Community work. It's its own little world up here."

She'd been expecting more buildings, barns or places

Julianne might be, but there was very little in the way structures out here.

"Where did they store things?" asked Austin, echoing her thoughts. "Seeds and machinery, crops, that sort of thing?"

"There's a big pole barn on the other side of the property, not far from the main house. That's where the equipment is kept. The crops used to go into the potato cellars up there on the hill."

Cassidy narrowed her eyes. "I don't see anything."

"Sure you do. See those five little hills all in a row?"

"Yes."

"That's them. They have concrete floors dug down in the earth and cinderblock walls. The roof is a big metal half-circle that can take the weight of the ground on top of it."

"You mean the potato cellar is underground?"

"That's right."

"What are they used for today?"

"I don't imagine I know."

"Can we take a closer look?" asked Austin.

Lucas clucked his tongue. "Unfortunately not. It's getting on lunchtime, and I need to get you back."

"But we haven't seen the whole property, have we?" asked Cassidy.

"The rest is just more fields, Sister Cassidy. Acres and acres of fields."

They headed back toward the main ranch. If Lucas was being truthful, there were only a handful of places that Julianne could be. The pole barn that held the equipment and the potato cellars.

Her shoulders shimmied just thinking about what Lucas described. A room built under the ground with a cement floor and no light. It would be damp and cold — perfect for potatoes, but not so perfect for people.

By the time they pulled in beside the dining hall, Cassidy knew she had to go back there and see for herself if her friend was inside one of those underground prisons.

16

"Senator Keaton Lane is here to see you, sir."

Jax scowled at the phone. He'd just talked to Mrs. Lane this morning, updating her on the situation with Cassidy. Austin's message should have reassured them. Cassidy had been found, was in the company of a HERO Force agent, and should be home soon, assuming all went well going forward.

"Show him into the conference room."

The senator must be worried. As a parent himself, Jax understood what it was like to have your heart separated from your body and walking around the earth, where anything could happen to it.

Violet was his world, the spitting image of her mother. He walked to the conference room thinking not for the first time about retiring from HERO Force completely. Since Cowboy had officially taken charge, it seemed Jax's presence here only serve to undermine the other man's authority. That was the last thing he wanted, and Cowboy certainly didn't need to be supervised.

The question was what Jax would do instead. He no

longer wanted to be in combat or dangerous situations. Jessa deserved more peace than that. Though he hadn't told anyone yet, she was pregnant again and his priorities were drifting farther and farther away from this place.

"Senator Lane." The other man was standing and Jax gestured to a chair. "Have a seat. I talked to your wife this morning."

"Yes. That's why I'm here." The recessed lights cast everything in a theater-like golden glow, highlighting the perspiration on the senator's head. "She wouldn't want me to be here talking to you. She doesn't need to know what I'm about to say."

Jax leaned back in his chair. "I'm listening."

"She said your man found Cassidy, but he's not bringing her home."

"That's right. Your daughter feels strongly that the other reporter, Julianne Garrison, is still alive."

"I see. So your man is letting her stay in harm's way?"

"That's one way to look at it, I suppose."

The senator punctuated his words with a pointed finger. "I hired you to bring her back safely. My daughter. Just mine. I didn't hire you to save the world."

Jax tapped his pencil eraser on the polished wooden table. "It's my understanding that it's Cassidy's desire to look for her friend that is keeping them at the compound. Not Austin's."

"I should have considered he might be loyal to her instead of me, given their history."

"And what history is that? You never said, exactly."

The older man pursed his lips, as if the answer to that question tasted sour and foul. "They were romantically involved. It was a long time ago. It isn't relevant today. But you have a responsibility to me as your client to get my daughter out of there as soon as possible, no matter what she wants."

Jax understood the senator's fear for his daughter's safety and his desire to get her back as soon as possible. And if the other man seemed hard and unconcerned with the other reporters safety, then perhaps that was just a father's instinctive desire to care for his own.

"Why didn't you want your wife to come with you today?"

The senator leaned back in his chair. "I told you. She wouldn't understand what I'm asking you to do. Typical female. She can't make a decision based on win versus loss. Acceptable casualties. She would have everyone die while she deliberated on how to save them all."

"You know there was an accident. I don't have constant contact with Austin at this time. He was able to reach us once, but it's not a phone call we can return and it doesn't mean we'll speak to him again."

"But you have other soldiers on the ground."

"Yes."

The senator leaned forward, pointing his finger again. "Then when they get there, you tell them the only life that matters is the one they were hired to save. Cassidy's. Not Julianne's."

17

Austin waited for Cassidy near the shower outside her dorm, hopeful she would know to look for him there. They hadn't gotten a chance to speak privately after lunch, though he knew she heard Austin asking David for permission to spend the night.

The weather had taken a turn for the worse with a late spring snowfall and whipping cold winds. David seemed less than thrilled, but as long as he obliged, Austin didn't care.

The sound of footsteps came toward him in the darkness. "I wasn't sure you'd be here," she said.

"We have to go check out those potato cellars."

"And the pole barn. How are we going to get out there?"

He took her hand and walked toward the main house. "I'm going to take Lucas's truck."

Lucas had parked it quite a distance from David's house, making Austin confident he could hot-wire it without being caught. "But this is it, Cassidy. We'll check the pole barn and the cellars, but then were leaving. Tonight."

"In the snow?"

"It isn't really a problem, I just told David it was. The tent will keep us warm and our supplies are suitable for any weather."

She nodded. "Okay. That's more than fair. I don't even know where else to look if she's not in one of those places, and I'm getting the feeling we're living on borrowed time."

"You noticed that, too?"

"David isn't going to stand for this much longer."

The truck wasn't locked. The interior light came on and Austin turned it off quickly, then got to hot-wiring the starter. It took some time, but soon they were off.

He drove slowly for the first hundred feet or so near the buildings and kept the truck's lights off, careful to keep his foot off the brake. The truck bounced once. "Must have been a pothole," he said.

He continued to move slowly as they got further from the main buildings, not wanting to alert anyone to their late-night drive, until something caught his eye in the rearview mirror. "We've got company."

"What? Who?"

"I don't know, but their lights are on and they're gaining on us."

"It has to be David, Lucas or Thomas. They are the only ones with access to vehicles. What are we going to do?"

"Hang on." He took off through an open field hoping the snow and darkness would hide them. "I have to go faster."

"But you can't see!"

"In my pack. Grab the night vision goggles. Quickly." He put them on and hit the gas, cruising full speed into the night.

Cassidy twisted around in her seat. "They're not following us. They can't see where we went."

Up ahead was a large tree separating one field from

another, and Austin was heading right for it. "I have to turn and I can't brake. Brace yourself." He took his foot off the gas, slowing the vehicle as much as he could, but he still needed to swerve to miss the outermost branches. Cassidy flew across the bench seat and into his side.

She was breathing hard. "This is scaring the shit out of me. It's like Space Mountain, that roller coaster at Disney World that's all in the dark."

"Roller coasters are fun."

"This is not fun, Austin!"

In the distance he saw the four hills Lucas had shown them earlier, the tops of the potato cellars. He steered toward them.

"Uh oh," said Cassidy. "Look over there."

Sure enough, the car that had been following them was headed for the potato cellars, too. "Wait a second," he said. "What if they aren't following us at all?"

"What else would they be doing out here at night like this?" She gasped. "Oh my God. Austin, they're going to see Julianne."

"Maybe. If she really is alive and she's out here someplace, they must be taking care of her." He took his foot off the gas, allowing the truck to slow down on its own. It came to a complete stop about four hundred feet from the hills. The other vehicle parked in front of the structures with its lights on.

They watched as someone in a coat and hat crossed in front of the headlight beams, then disappeared on the other side of the cellar hills.

"Can you tell who it is?" he asked.

"No."

Austin put the truck in park. "I'm going to get closer so I can get a better look." He reached for his pack, withdrawing a firearm and loading a magazine, then tucking another in his pocket.

"Be careful," she said.

She sat in the cab of the truck trying to see where he'd gone, but quickly lost him in the snow and darkness. She felt safe in that moment, knowing Austin the Navy SEAL was there to protect her.

He was such a strong force in her life, and in the world in general. She was certain if Julianne was alive and on this property, he would find her.

I still love that man.

The thought made her choked up. Would she never learn? Never protect her heart? He wanted to see her again. Wanted a second chance. It was so tempting, her heart and her body wanting him so much, but her mind knew better. He'd hurt her before and he would hurt her again.

The driver's side door opened.

"That was quick," she said as he slid in beside her.

Lucas turned and faced her. "That's funny. It seemed like I was back there forever."

Cassidy screamed loudly. Lucas punched her in the jaw and she stopped, shocked by the pain that exploded across her face.

"That's Thomas over there," he said. "Do you want him to know you're here?"

"No. Please don't tell him."

"I won't if I don't have to. I'm sorry I hit you." He shook his hand out. "You shouldn't be here, Sister Cassidy. If he finds out, he'll be real angry."

"How did you find us?"

"I saw the light come on in my truck so I came outside just in time to see you two driving away. I hopped in the back." He gestured toward the field that separated them from the potato cellars. "You have no business snooping around out here. What are you doing, for heaven's sake?"

Lies popped into her mind, not one of them remotely convincing. She opened her mouth, not sure what she would say. She was as surprised as Lucas when the truth came out. "I'm looking for Julianne."

Lucas's eyes shot to hers in the darkened cab.

"You know who she is. I can see it in your face. You remember her."

He looked away.

"She's my friend. She's the nicest, kindest, gentlest human being I've ever known, and she went missing from this place."

"Is that why you came to The Community? To look for your friend?"

"Yes. You could help me, Lucas. You could tell me what happened to her. You could help me find her and bring her home to her family. Everyone is so worried about her, and you could help."

"There is no Julianne. Not anymore."

Her face crumpled. "Is she dead?"

"Are you a reporter, too?"

"Yes."

Lucas reached inside his coat, withdrawing a firearm. Cassidy stared at it, transfixed. "Lucas, please..."

"It has a silencer. Top of the line model from Finland." He sighed heavily. "Brother David has the ear of the Lord."

"No. He's hurting people. He won't let anyone leave. God wouldn't tell him to do that."

"God told him to kill Julianne."

She gasped. "Is that what happened to her?"

"No." He turned his head to face her. "He had me do it instead."

She reached for the handle to open the door, fear and panic exploding in her veins, but he was too fast. He wrapped his arm around her neck and pulled her against his chest. "Stop fighting me," he said.

"Let me go!" she yanked her arm back, stabbing him in the solar plexus with her elbow. He grunted but kept hold of her neck.

"Listen to me."

"She was pregnant," she said. "She was a good person and you killed her." She aimed lower this time, sinking down as low as she could before striking him in the scrotum.

"Ah!" This time he let her go. In the darkness she fumbled for the door handle, finally grasping it and opening it to the outside, an icy blast of air coming into the cab of the truck. "Your friend is alive," he said.

She spun around, the snow nearly making her slip. "Is that a trick?"

"I could shoot you right now, but I have not. I wouldn't kill her and I won't kill you, either." He put the gun on the dash. "She might be better off dead than the way she's living." He stared at the car in the distance with its lights on. "That's my fault, too."

Understanding dawned, horrible and shocking. "Thomas is in there with her."

"Yes." He keened like a small child about to sob. "He found out what I'd done, that I let her live. I knew about the baby. It didn't seem right to kill her." He took a shuddering breath. "I thought for sure he would tell Brother David, but instead he started...hurting her. He knew I couldn't tell anyone. Until you. You can stop Thomas. You can save her."

"You have to help us get her out of here."

He nodded. "Close the door. I'll be right there."

She shut it quietly and turned toward the potato cellars. A sound like a big rock hitting pavement came from inside the car, making her jump. "No, no, no!" She opened the door and peered inside, her head jerking back at what she saw, blood and gore and horror.

She slammed it closed.

Where was Austin? She wanted to scream for him, to call out and run, but the blowing wind, fluttering snow and headlights in the distance were all she could see. She was crying, tears running down her face. Lucas had shot himself.

Lucas was dead.

"Austin," she called quietly into the field. She moved through the cold night air, hugging her arms to her chest. Julianne was in that building, probably being raped by Thomas. And somewhere nearby, the only man who could help her stop this nightmare was hiding in the darkness, watching it all unfold.

18

The short end of each potato cellar ended in a wooden side, the aged planks painted pale blue and fitted with a double barn door. The cellar doors the man had gone through were directly in front of the car with the headlights shining, and the sides and top of the cellar were covered with several feet of earth, making it impossible for Austin to get close without being detected.

But he needed to find a way, because a woman was screaming from inside the cellar.

He was perched behind the man's car, gun drawn, weighing his options. Every muscle in his body wanted to burst forth and propel him forward into that space, knowing someone was experiencing a terrible situation. But the tactical reality was he had no idea of knowing what awaited him on the other side.

"Austin."

He turned to find Cassidy walking toward him through the snow. Her voice was raspy and she sounded like she'd been crying. He stood. "Be quiet. There's someone in there."

The woman screamed again, a plaintive sound like an injured animal.

"Julianne!" Cassidy whispered. "We have to help her. It's Thomas. I think he's raping her. Lucas was in the truck—"

"*What?*"

"He stowed away in the back when we first came out here. Julianne is alive. He couldn't kill her like David asked him to, but Thomas found out and he's been hurting her. We have to help her." She moved toward the building but Austin hauled her back.

"Where is Lucas now?"

"Dead. He shot himself in the truck."

Her eyes were wide like saucers, her reaction oddly mechanical. She was in shock.

"If we go in there, we'll have to kill him," he said.

"Let me do it." She reached for his gun.

"Wait, Cassidy."

"I'm tired of waiting. Don't you hear her screaming? He's hurting her, Austin. We have to do something."

He nodded. "Agreed, but we have to make sure he doesn't have the upper hand. He could use her as a shield if we're not careful." He pulled a knife from a pocket in his pants, handing it to her. "I have a smoke grenade, but it will blind us just as effectively as it will him. Not going to use that unless I have to."

"Let me help."

He assessed her coolly. "Combat is different than anything you've experienced. Take the knife and go to the car. Keep yourself out of harm's way."

"But what if you need me?"

"Go, Cassidy." A light in the distance behind her caught his eye. Another set of headlights. "Fuck." He gestured to the approaching vehicle. "If Lucas is dead and Thomas is in the cellar..."

"That's David."

"Don't go to the car. Hide in the next potato cellar. We have to do this, now."

She nodded and jogged away. Austin pulled his night vision goggles back into place and approached the double doors, the peaceful snowfall contrasting with the violence he heard within.

He slid one of the doors open, light flooding the space from the headlights outside. There was a naked woman on an angled conveyer belt, a man on top of her, turning to stare at Austin.

"Get off her," he said.

"Get out of here, Lucas, you simpleton. I'm just having some fun."

Austin fired a shot into the cellar, deliberately missing them. Thomas hopped up, holding up his hands until his pants fell completely down, showing his limp erection. He grabbed the pants with one hand, the other still raised.

"Lucas is dead," said Austin. "He killed himself because of his part in what you're doing here."

"You're the man who brought Sister Cassidy back to The Community."

"I'm the man who's taking Julianne back home. Step away from her."

"I'm unarmed. Don't shoot." Thomas moved over and Julianne came down from the conveyer belt, stumbling when her feet hit the ground. Austin moved instinctually to catch her, his gun shifting as he did.

Pain sliced through Austin's hand and thigh and he dropped his weapon, dots on his goggles that could only be blood. He looked down to see a throwing star sticking out of his quadriceps—three blades out, two blades in. It had gone through part of his hand on its way to his leg.

He'd underestimated Thomas, assuming the half-naked man was unarmed and allowing his attention to be distracted by the limping Julianne. He must have grabbed the star from a pocket when he pulled up his pants.

Austin bent down and reached for his weapon, the motion of his thigh muscle further deepening the wound, and he lost his balance. Thomas moved to run by him out the cellar doors.

A warrior's cry sounded behind him as Cassidy took Thomas down with a karate kick and a fierce jab to his eyes. He fell to the ground just as Austin yanked the throwing star from his leg and picked up his weapon. He turned back to Thomas, not believing what he saw.

Blood spurted from Thomas's throat, the knife Austin had given her clenched tightly in her hand. He had already been incapacitated, but Cassidy decided Thomas needed to die. Her eyes met Julianne's across the room. "He'll never hurt you again."

Julianne cried quietly. "Thank you."

Austin looked outside. The car he'd seen from a great distance was now just moments away. "Come," he barked. "We'll take Thomas's car and leave The Community."

Cassidy moved to his side. "He's too close."

"I can get away from him. Get in the car."

"We'll never make it. I'm staying here."

"What?"

"David won't hurt me. You come back for me when you can. I'll keep him from chasing you out of the compound."

She still had that eerie demeanor, made worse now by the blood on her hands and shirt.

"You're in shock. You don't know what you're saying. Get in the damn car, Cassidy."

Julianne walked between them and got in the vehicle.

Cassidy backed away from Austin, her top now glowing in David's approaching headlights. "I love you," she said.

He took two steps toward her, pain shooting up his leg from the motion. "I'm not leaving you here."

"Look at her," she whispered. "She needs your help. You can drive fast with your night vision. You can get away. It's me he wants, baby." She moved to touch her face, but stopped herself. "I can make this okay." She backed father away from him, the lights now even more intense.

"No!"

"Goodbye, Austin." She turned toward the car, waving her arms.

Time stood still. She was out of his reach, refusing the shelter of his protection. He could grab her. Pick her up. Throw her in the car.

And David would follow.

He turned abruptly and got in the car, lowering his goggles and speeding off before David arrived. He stared at his rearview mirror, watching as her silhouette was absorbed into the light like a moth burning up in a flame.

19

Austin stretched his good leg out beside the fire while Noah stitched up the gashes on his hand. The newest member of HERO Force had sewn up Austin's leg first, which was why he wasn't moving it anywhere.

The fire felt good, first for the heat, second for what it symbolized. They were no longer hiding from David Kelleher. As far as Austin was concerned, they were hunters taking a break before going back for the kill, and the reversal of their roles had his blood pumping.

He was tense as hell knowing Cassidy was in there with that psychopath by herself while all the good guys with guns were on this side of the perimeter, and he wished again she'd come with him instead of sacrificing herself at the potato cellars.

Noah handed him a full canteen. "You might want to wash off some of the blood. I'm done with the stitches."

"Thanks." He poured some on his leg, rubbing at the dried blood that seemed to be everywhere. "You didn't sign your initials. Not into showing off your handiwork?"

Noah chuckled. "Not this time. When you need a full appendectomy in the field, that's when I get creative."

The sound of a helicopter could be heard in the distance. HERO Force, come to pick up Julianne. The men exchanged a look. She'd been in bad shape, suffering from extreme dehydration and malnutrition in addition to the trauma from the rape.

"I'm worried she might lose the baby. I'm bringing in the bird," Cowboy had said.

"The compound will be able to hear it," said Noah.

"I don't give a fuck. Think of it as war drums beating on the wind, letting them know what's about to come roaring through their asshole."

He was upset about Julianne. They all were. They could handle their own blood and guts being spilled on the floor and sewn up with a needle and thread, but seeing a young pregnant woman in that kind of condition had shaken them to the core.

Cowboy had found a clearing nearby for the helicopter to land, then carried her there when she'd barely been able to stand. Austin and Noah had been somber in their wake.

"I should turn around and go back in there right now," said Austin. He was staring into the flames, his conscience blaming him for anything and everything that might be happening to Cassidy.

Noah dug in his pack, pulling out a pill bottle and shaking some out. "You lost a lot of blood. Stay here the night and get some sleep. We'll kick some ass in the morning." He held out his hand to Austin.

"No thanks." He deserved to feel this pain. The last thing he wanted was something to take the edge off.

"Antibiotics."

Austin took the pills and washed them down with water.

The sound of the helicopter taking off could be heard through the trees.

"That was a pretty stupid thing you did, going into the compound by yourself," said Noah.

"Wasn't so smart of you two to get your chutes tangled at eight hundred feet."

"That was Logan."

"I figured as much. He okay?"

"Broke his femur. And his pride. Fucking lucky to be alive."

Austin hissed. "Ouch."

"Going to be at least six months until it's healed."

"I'm sure Charlotte will make sure he gets his exercise sitting down." He took a long drink of water. "You did a good job with Logan."

"What, falling from the sky?"

"I know you must have grabbed him or there's no way he'd be alive right now."

"Yeah, well, I dropped him when I hit the tree line."

"That's just so he learns for next time." The men laughed. "Seriously man, I was there, and I thought he was going to bounce."

"Yeah. I thought that for a minute myself, even after I grabbed hold of him."

Noah gave the first MRE to Austin, then heated up a second. The food, the water, and the warmth were making him feel sated and sleepy—unless Noah was right and he really had lost that much blood. He stared at his tent already setup and waiting for him, remembering how he'd made love to Cassidy inside it.

She'd told him she loved him right before he left, and he hadn't said a goddamn thing. She was dazed and in shock. The words didn't mean anything when they were spoken like that, but the memory made his chest tighten regardless.

It was possible she really did love him, and he thought of those war drums on the air—this time foretelling of heartache and loss just like he'd experienced the first time he tried to love her. Nothing had changed since then. They'd only had time to know what they'd been missing and how good they'd been together. Shit, that just made it worse. Because there was no way in hell he and Cassidy Lane could ever be more than lovers.

Cowboy appeared through the trees. "She's a fucking mess," he said. "The medics were acting like she was about to code." He held his hands over the fire, shaking his head. "I wanted to take a picture while they were hooking her up to the monitors and send it to Senator Lane, just so he'd have something to think about when he's trying to sleep at night."

Austin cocked his head. "What are you talking about?"

"He showed up at the office to see Jax. He wanted to remind us we were hired to save his daughter and his daughter only, that if there was a choice between the two women he would be highly disappointed if we chose Julianne."

"That is fucked up," said Austin. "I mean I get it, you want Cassidy to be all right. But that makes it sound like the other person was just expendable to him."

"Exactly," said Cowboy. "He even went on about collateral damage and how sometimes you've got to sacrifice one life to save another. You would think that son of a bitch wanted her to die in there, for how much concern he showed."

Noah shook his head. "Somebody did want her to die in there. Telling David Kelleher she was a spy posing as a follower was akin to a death sentence. It's a miracle she got out of there alive."

Austin furrowed his brow. "The bloody press credentials and necklace... the ones Lane showed us as 'proof' Julianne was dead? Why would Kelleher send those to the *Post*?"

"A warning," said Cowboy. "Reporters die here."

"No. He's an isolationist. He let a freaking road become overgrown with trees because he doesn't like contact with the outside world. Sending that press pass was like waving a red flag in front of one of the biggest bulls in the media today."

"He didn't do it," said Noah.

"Then who the fuck did?" asked Cowboy.

"Somebody who wanted it to look like Julianne was dead," said Austin.

"Maybe so we don't go looking for Julianne instead of Cassidy." said Cowboy.

Austin's mind raced. "But what's so wrong about saving Julianne?"

"That's the four-million-dollar question, right there," said Noah.

"How many people knew she was in there, do you think?" asked Austin. "Her boss. Maybe her coworkers."

"Friends, family," said Cowboy.

"The father of her child," said Noah.

"One of them had to have revealed Julianne's identity to David Kelleher."

"The baby's father," said Austin. He looked from Cowboy to Noah. "Are you thinking what I'm thinking?"

Cowboy and Noah answered at the same time. "Senator Lane."

"Cassidy probably introduced them." Austin shook his

head. "It could have ruined his career—his marriage, if that got out."

"No better way for an affair to be advertised than with a baby," said Cowboy.

"Is this really possible?" asked Noah.

Cowboy pulled out his satellite phone. "I know how to find out. I'm going to ask him."

20

C assidy thought she might be losing her mind after killing a man yesterday. She stared at her reflection. She wore a long white dress, simple, plain and utterly terrifying. Her head looked disconnected from her body, as if she truly failed to recognize herself.

David was insisting she was ready to take her vow.

It's not like he was giving her any choice in the matter, but she didn't see the point in explaining to him how that negated any value in taking the vow at all. He was acting more strangely today than in the whole time she'd been here at Longwood Ranch, talking to himself and swatting at imaginary bees around his face.

Her eyes went to the clock. It was early—only six in the morning—and he was pushing her to hurry up. He paced behind her. "We need to complete your commitment ceremony before we leave for Seattle."

"Why?"

He looked at her like she was the crazy one. "So you can be my bride."

The last twelve hours were a blur. She'd stood in the

shower for what seemed an eternity letting the water carry Thomas's blood down the drain, wondering all the while how Austin had fared with his wounds from David's throwing star and if Julianne and the baby would be all right.

She'd all but fallen into bed only to be awakened several hours later by a woman from The Community holding the white dress, claiming to be there for a fitting.

It was still dark outside at the time.

But it was the helicopter that really pushed David over the edge. He shouted to himself in barely intelligible ramblings about doomsday and God's revenge against the sinners and nonbelievers.

He stopped just as suddenly as he'd begun, only to peer at her strangely. "You're all that I have now."

"You've been through a lot in the last two days, David. We don't need to go to Seattle today. You should rest."

He stormed across the room to her. "Do you think the wrath of a God scorned can wait?" He backhanded her across the face.

She held her aching cheek, still sore from when Lucas hit her the night before to stop her screaming.

"Come now. It's time for your vow." When she didn't stand up immediately he grabbed her by the hair and pulled her to a stand, holding her in front of his body. "You're going to look so beautiful dangling from the Space Needle."

Her mouth dropped open. Could he really mean what he'd just said? David was bizarre and he clearly had psychological problems, but she never thought he was quite this mad. She couldn't even imagine he was sincere. "What are you talking about? Let me go."

He held on tightly. "A spectacle of biblical proportions.

The sacrificial virgin hanging close to death, only to be pulled back to safety by the suffering of sinners."

The look in his eye could only be described as joyful. Terror unlike any she'd ever known flashed through her body like an electrical pulse. "You're scaring me."

"You should know God's wrath. Then you will be afraid."

"God is good. He's loving and kind."

"That's what sinners tell themselves." He let her go abruptly. Her hands were shaking.

He narrowed his eyes, as if searching for some flaw in her face. "Come to the porch. I have the font waiting."

He really believes he's talking to God. He's really going to do this.

Was it possible? The Space Needle had to have tons of security. He couldn't just take her out there and...

Her train of thought made her physically ill. She couldn't finish.

She followed him begrudgingly through the house and onto the back porch. A marble birdbath filled with water sat in the center, a golden pitcher inside it.

The font. Like a baptism.

Except this guy's a certifiable loony who wants to kill me, instead of a priest.

She felt the unfortunate need to giggle at the absurdity of the situation and she bit down hard on her tongue to keep from laughing.

There wasn't anything funny about this.

In that moment she missed Austin so intensely she wouldn't have been surprised if he could feel it across time and space. Her mouth pulled down hard at the corners. He was gone and he wasn't coming back.

Not in time, anyway.

For a moment she allowed herself to feel self-pity,

wishing she'd been the one to escape. But even as she had the thought she replayed her decision from last night in her mind and knew she'd make the same one a hundred times over again.

Julianne was safe. She was with Austin and he would protect her. Maybe he'd come back for her before David took her away.

He could be nearby right now, just waiting to make his move. Or had he taken Julianne down the mountain? The helicopter surely must have been from them and she prayed Austin hadn't been on it, hadn't left her so completely. She squeezed her eyes shut.

He said he'd come back for you.

David pointed at the deck beside the birdbath. "Kneel."

She was sobbing openly now. Her knees hit the wood deck hard. Surely it would leave bruises. Everything was experiencing was bound to leave it's mark on her forever, and she only hoped she would survive.

He put his hand on her head, his fingertips pressing too hard into her scalp, and she tied to pull away from him.

"Hold still!" he said.

Austin. Where are you?

David poured icy water over her head, drenching her clothes and face. David pet her head like a dog and she cried harder.

"Look at me," he said, his breath foul and directly in front of her. She kept her face turned away. He yanked her hair harder. "Look at me!"

She met his eyes, the look in his like pure evil. "Do you Cassidy Lane vow to become one with The Community? To consider the needs of the group before your own, and to do God's bidding, no matter how difficult?"

She crossed her fingers behind her back like a child telling a lie and said a silent prayer.

Please forgive me. I don't know what else to do.

21

Austin swerved through traffic in downtown Seattle, Cowboy in the passenger seat and the radio playing in the background. The city was Armageddon. The final showdown between good and evil was well under way, people running along the sidewalks, cars swerving madly to escape.

It was chaos.

Four bombs had gone off in Seattle that day, all in heavily crowded public places. The first had been at the Pike Place Market with casualties numbering more than twenty, including young children.

He had to get to Cassidy before something happened to her. He'd once let her slip from his life as easily as sand through his fingers. Now he desperately needed to keep her in it.

He wouldn't let himself imagine life without her. Not now. Not after he knew how much she meant to him. Not ever again.

"Another bomb has gone off, this one in the aquarium, sending millions of gallons of water through the crowded structure. At

least five people are confirmed dead. That number's expected to rise."

"Son of a bitch," Austin said. "Why hasn't he made a statement? If he's not going to tell the public why he's doing this, what's the fucking point?"

"Maybe he's like the Son of Sam," said Cowboy. "The voices are making him do it."

Austin and the others went back to Longwood Ranch at dawn but David and Cassidy were already gone. Austin felt like his entire world was slipping off its axis, about to tumble through space. He looked for The Community's helicopter.

It was gone.

He'd taken her.

David had taken Cassidy.

Austin shattered a window with a single kick, his emotions under pressure and needing to escape.

Where the hell had they gone?

As soon as he posed the question he knew the answer, his memory pulling up the map of Seattle from David's office.

He could only remember a few of the places marked. The Space Needle. Pike Place Market. The Great Wheel.The Art Museum.

And the aquarium, apparently.

He wished he'd paid more attention or written them down, and he berated himself during the whole chopper ride to Seattle for failing to realize the map's importance. It had been spread out before him and he'd damn near ignored it.

He swerved to miss a Toyota stopped in the middle of the busy street, no driver in sight, as he spoke to Cowboy. "Where the fuck is she? He brought her here, but I can't imagine he dragged her all over town setting charges."

"That could have been done weeks or days ago by any member of The Community," said Cowboy.

"He's here to watch his masterpiece as it unfolds," said Austin. "He needs to be part of it. Needs to see it with his own eyes."

"He might even need to be a part of it."

"But where? That's the question. It's a big city and we've got nothing to go on."

"Cassidy Lane, a reporter from the Washington Post, *is believed to be with The Community and has issued a statement on their behalf. It reads, 'The people of Seattle must repent their sinister ways. More people will die before the fires of hell are cleared from the earth, and only the righteous will be guided through the darkness as if on rails.'"*

"'As if on rails,'" Cowboy said. "That's awkward as hell."

It really was, but Cassidy was a journalist. She could write better than that. Going through the darkness on rails reminded him of his earlier conversation with Cassidy about the roller coaster Space Mountain at Disneyworld. His eyes widened. "It's deliberate. It's a clue for me."

Cowboy turned toward him. "Come again?"

"We were talking about Space Mountain the other day. She knew my mind would go right there."

Noah chimed in from the backseat. "I hate that ride. The whole thing's in the dark. You never know when the turns are coming."

"I don't know about you," said Cowboy, "But when I'm trying to decide between major Seattle attractions, Space Mountain makes me think of Space Needle."

"Me too," said Austin and Noah at the same time.

Austin pulled over and cut people off making a U-turn

in chaotic Doomsday traffic. "That's where he's taking her. The Space Needle."

It was a incredibly tall tower in downtown Seattle known for its circular observation deck overlooking the city, Elliott Bay, and several mountains in the distance.

22

Cassidy stumbled up hundreds of stairs, David pulling her behind him. The elevator was closed, security and the police presence working to keep people out of the building. The longer she climbed, the sicker she was just knowing how high they must be and the terrible fate David had in store for her.

She couldn't stop thinking about it, the image of her hanging from the top of the Space Needle activating her fear of heights and nearly paralyzing her body, but he continued to drag her with him up higher and higher.

Her legs ached and her breath was coming fast, but the only sign David was affected by the difficulty of climbing hundreds of feet into the air was the perspiration saturating his underarms and back.

The elevators had been closed, guards posted at each bay. That didn't stop David, though. He'd walked through a back service entrance and straight into a stairwell as if he were invisible to the masses. He believed God was helping him, but Cassidy was damn sure that wasn't the case. He'd been lucky, and she could only hope his luck would run out soon.

She tripped and went down on her knee, the solid step unforgiving as it hit bone, and she gasped. "Slow down. You're hurting me."

"You're not going fast enough. We're on a very strict schedule. I don't want too much time between the explosion at the market and what I have planned here, or the networks will go back to regular programming. Fucking heathens! You can never miss your soap operas or game shows. Not even for God."

She clenched her jaw, her physical fatigue and fear making her brave in the face of this man. "You aren't God."

She was still on her knees on the stairs when David lifted his leg and kicked her in the ribs. "I may not be God, but I am as good as God to you. Now get up."

Nausea was bubbling through her abdomen and she clutched at her side, unmoving. In one swift movement he brought his knee within a fraction of an inch of her already throbbing jawbone.

"Get up!"

With a strength she didn't know she had, she pulled herself to a stand. David grabbed her hand and resumed his march, dragging her in tow. This time as they passed the window, her gaze swept the horrifying view.

So. High. Up.

She bent at the waist and threw up, barely missing her dress. David yanked her forward through the mess.

He started blabbering again, nonsensical words mixed in with talk of damnation and fire. He seemed to be losing his connection with reality and every way that mattered—every way except the planning of his attacks.

She yanked her hand out of his. "I'm not going."

"Yes, you are."

"Beat me." She shrugged. "I don't care anymore. You can't make me go up there."

He grabbed another fistful of her hair and pulled hard, her scalp already so tender from the last time he'd done so. "I'll bet I can."

"Try it. If you want me to hang me off the top of this thing, you'll have to kill me before we get there."

He narrowed his eyes. "You're going to help me convince this city of sinners to repent and change their ways. Don't you want that?"

"I don't really give a shit." She turned around, aware of her exaggerated movements like a drunk person. The first blow shouldn't have been a surprise, but it was. He slammed her head into the wall with such force she thought he might have killed her right then.

She continued to move down the stairway as David ranted, his footfalls heavy on the steps behind her. "Of course, none of them will do it. It's already too late for them. It's the example we're setting for the others that matters."

He kicked her in the back, sending her flying down the steps and headfirst into the landing, her white polyester dress sticking to her skin like a mummy's wrap.

Austin isn't coming. He isn't going to save you.

She was dizzy and in so much pain, consciousness no longer a given. She tried to focus her eyes as David reached around her waist and picked her up, putting her over his shoulder.

The motion of his body as he carried her worsened her dizziness and nausea. "Stupid girl," he said with a snicker. "If you were going to resist, you should have done it at the bottom of the stairway, not the top."

She must have blacked out, because when she came to,

she was sitting on the landing beside a door and he was strapping something on her face. She pawed at it.

"It's a gas mask. Unless you'd truly like to die?"

She reluctantly pulled it onto her face. Dying was seeming like more and more of a possibility today. She thought of her parents and how upset they would be. She thought of Austin's face when she'd refused to leave the compound with him. If she'd only known it would be the last time she'd see his face, she would have told him what was in her heart.

I love him.

He opened the door to the observation deck a mere few inches and threw something out of the stairwell. Voices erupted in a cacophony of panic from the other side of the door. Someone tried to open the stairwell door but David fought to keep it closed, the woman on the other side coughing heavily until there was no noise at all.

David turned to Cassidy, pushed his gas mask to the top of his head and smiled. "Are you ready for your big moment?"

You're going to look so beautiful dangling from the Space Needle.

She took in a shaking breath and keened, her eyes squeezing shut. A voice in her head shouted for her to be brave, not to let this man see he'd broken her, but hysteria had taken hold and all she could do was cry.

She couldn't imagine he was serious until now, would never believe he was capable of pulling off such a stunt until now— police officers unconscious on the other side of the door, the crazed look in his eye that said everything was going as planned.

Stop your sniveling and fight back!

This psychotic fucker had a God complex, and it was

high time she knocked some holes in his theories. She ripped off her mask. "I'm not going to let you do this. You have no power over me."

He raised his chin. "You vowed your loyalty to me and The Community."

"I lied. You are not God. I have free will and I can do as I please."

His eyes went wide. "I am your destiny. You are the pure woman I was promised."

She laughed out loud. "I am not a virgin, you asshole. So if you're looking for some sacrificial lamb to hang off the Space Needle like a spider on a string, you're plum out of luck."

He spit on her face, in her eye, in her mouth. "The devil can have you then, but the show must go on."

23

"We have to get up there," said Cowboy, flashing his identification to the policeman guarding the elevator that ran to the top of the Space Needle.

"HERO Force?" said the officer, handing back his ID. "Only official government agency responders can go upstairs."

"Leo Wilson, U.S. Navy SEAL. This is Austin Dixon and Noah Ryker. They're SEALs, too. We've been working undercover at The Community, a cult run by David Kelleher."

The officer's eyes widened. "The guy blowing up the bombs."

"That's right. We have reason to believe he's on the observation deck with a hostage."

"The observation deck was cleared more than an hour ago. The only people up there are law enforcement."

Austin and Cowboy exchanged a glance. "Check," said Austin.

The officer furrowed his brow. "Excuse me?"

Cowboy shrugged. "You guys have security cameras up there, don't you? Check the feed. If there is nothing abnormal, we'll leave you alone with our apologies."

The cop looked to another cop, who shrugged. "Why not?"

"All right, I'll go check. You two stay here." He pointed at the other policemen. "Don't let them upstairs."

He walked away and Cowboy moved closer to Austin, whispering, "What if everything up there is fine?"

"Then we go to plan B."

"Which is what?"

"I don't have a fucking clue."

A ruckus erupted from the street, the noise reaching them through two banks of glass doors. Austin and Cowboy ran outside, one voice standing out against the others. "Someone's hanging from the observation deck!" shouted a man.

Austen feared what he would find before he even raised his head. There, hanging some hundred feet in the air from the bottom of the space needle, was a woman in a white dress.

A woman who could only be Cassidy.

Horror like nothing he'd ever experienced pulled a cry of pure fear from his gut as the moment moved in slow motion. "No!"

Then he was racing back inside, Cowboy on his heels. The officer who'd gone to look at the surveillance footage waved them into the elevator, three officers already inside. "Everybody on the observation floor is down," said the cop as the doors closed. "We don't know if they are incapacitated or dead. The only person visible on the cameras is a man, forty to forty-five, small build, dark hair, climbing on the security cables."

"David Kelleher," said Austin. "There's a woman hanging from the observation deck. Cassidy Lane. We have to get her down safely." He pulled out his weapon as Cowboy and the officers did the same.

The car shot upward, the city of Seattle spread out before them through the glass walls.

"You know her?" asked the officer.

"Yes." He loaded the gun. "I'm the one who left her in harm's way."

This time you have to save her.

A dark abyss of self-doubt had opened in his mind. What if he couldn't get to her in time? What if the Space Needle was already wired to explode like the other attractions and Cassidy met her end along with it?

He had to keep it from happening.

The officer handed out gas masks. Moments ticked by like hours as they made their ascent, the doors finally opening onto a glass-walled round room with a walkway visible beyond it.

The observation deck. Somewhere out there was David Kelleher and—God willing—the tether that was keeping Cassidy from falling to the ground. Austin sprung forth, his gun at the ready as he made his way outside.

Cowboy went one way around the circle, Noah the other.

But the observation deck appeared to be empty. Austin ran three-quarters of the way around before finding Cowboy leaning out where Cassidy was suspended. The metal security ropes had been cut, allowing Kelleher to climb out of the observation deck and onto the steel that extended beyond it, the metal coming out like spokes that connected to a wider steel ring encompassing the tower.

There, around the outermost ring of the tower, was a

metal cable wrapped around and hanging down. Austin looked down, just able to see Cassidy's dress blowing in the breeze, his stomach turning as he grasped the depth of her plight.

"They have to have harnesses and safety cables here somewhere. Ask the cops. Go. Go!" he said to Cowboy, who hurried off.

Austin grabbed the broken cables and hauled himself up. He was so desperate to reach her a part of him longed to go out there now without a safety cable. A stupid move when Kelleher was around. As if on cue, a voice came from behind him.

"Welcome to the show."

Austin whipped around to find Kelleher behind him, smiling widely. He wore a body harness but had no weapon, and Austin longed to shoot him dead.

Or kill him with my bare hands.

He did neither.

Kelleher looked at the gun. "You don't want to do that. You see this?" In his hand he held what looked like a remote control device. "If I let go of this button, she'll plummet to the ground like a stone."

The officers who rode up with them in the elevator were visible in the glassed-in observation room behind Kelleher, carrying what must be harnesses and safety cables. Austin held up his hand to keep them there.

"Let her go, Kelleher."

"God wants her to dance. Right now every TV camera in town is pointed at that woman held high above the ground, hoping with all their might she survives." He pointed to the highest level of the Space Needle, a miniature observation deck just below the needle that looked like a maintenance area. "Today I will give my sermon on the mount, and all the eyes of the sinners in this city will see the error of their ways."

"What about Cassidy?"

"She'll die. That's the only way this story can end. True repentance only comes when something important is taken away."

"And the Space Needle?"

"It will explode with such force, the top will end up in Elliot Bay. Very dramatic for our friends in the media."

"And you die a martyr's death."

David cocked his head. "I live another day to teach others about the dangers of sin and greed. I am doing the Lord's work. He doesn't want me to perish."

"This God of yours sounds like a really nasty character."

"Those who don't believe are the worst sinners of all."

"Oh, I believe in God," said Austin. "I know he's real. But he's not the asshole you seem to think he is."

Kelleher's eyes darkened. "When the fires of hell lick at your feet, you will remember this moment."

"Like you, when this building explodes?"

"I told you, I will not die."

Austin narrowed his eyes. Half the world was downstairs, yet this man planned to escape? "Then how are you going to get out?"

"I'll spread my wings like an angel and fly."

Suddenly, a chorus of voices could be heard screaming from the street below, Cassidy's distinctive and louder yelp reaching Austin's ears. He responded viscerally, every hair on his body standing on end. "What did you do?" he growled as he looked over the edge. There was Cassidy, still hanging from the tower.

"Oops," said David. "My finger slipped. Now stay here or I'll really drop her next time."

"What's the matter?" asked Austin. "You afraid I'll show the crowd the good in humanity by going out on a limb to save another?"

"She's a whore and a temptress. She deserves to die for her sins."

"She's the woman I love." The words came so easily to his lips, yet they sounded strange to his ears. He'd never claimed to love a woman in his whole damn life.

It's true. I do love her.

And now he was in danger of losing her forever.

David scoffed.

Austin took a step toward him. "You wouldn't know about love, would you? You're damaged goods. Not right in the head. A psycho. What's the matter, mom and dad didn't love you enough?"

"Stop moving."

"You been called that before, David? Maybe you don't really talk to God. Maybe you just need a prescription."

"It doesn't matter. It's time for me to preach the truth to all the world. You tell those cops in there to let me through. Any funny business and the girl dies."

Austin walked ahead of him into the building, telling everyone to steer clear—the three cops, Cowboy and Noah. Kelleher produced a key and unlocked a door labelled, "Authorized Personnel Only."

"Remember," he said to Austin. "Try to rescue the girl and she'll be nothing but a splat on the sidewalk."

The door closed behind him.

"I found a firehose," said Noah. "Should be long enough to reach her."

"I'll climb out to the ring," said Austin.

"Here's your safety harness," said an officer.

Austin frowned. "What does it attach to?"

"There's an inner ring that goes around the whole structure. Made for safety lines for routine maintenance."

"But if she's hanging from the outside ring and I'm hanging from the inside, I won't be able to reach her."

The officer in charge spoke up. "He'll be able to see you if you go out to the rings."

Austin wanted to scream that he didn't care what Kelleher did to him as long as Cassidy was safe, but of course, he couldn't guarantee her safety if Kelleher saw him trying to save her. "What do you suggest?" asked Austin.

"The elevator shaft is directly beneath us. He won't be able to see you there. You still won't be that close to her, but you can push off from the structure and swing out to grab her. Plus he won't be able to see you from the top of the needle." The officer gestured to the doorway where Kelleher had just gone.

"Make it happen," said Austin.

One of the other officers stepped forward, holding a smartphone. "He's on the news. I don't know how he's broadcasting from here, but he's on the news, right on top of the Needle."

Austin took the phone, the others crowding around to see. Sure enough, there was Kelleher on what looked like a ten-foot deck atop the Space Needle.

"*...Today you have seen a tiny fraction of God's wrath. You must repent for your actions that offend him...*"

"Show me how to get to the elevator shaft," Austin said.

The officers led the way, Noah with the firehose in tow, Cowboy with the live news broadcast of David's apocalyptic prophecies. With the help of a crowbar from the maintenance closet, they managed to pry open the doors to an empty elevator bay, a cold, wet breeze blowing up from the abyss.

"Cowboy, get a safety harness. You're going to help me."

The officers rigged Austin to a steel eyehole in a beam with a twenty-foot metal cable. "I'll lower myself down, then Cowboy will follow." He turned to Cowboy. "You hang on to me while they unhook my security rope, then we find a new anchor and continue on."

Noah piped up. "The news is estimating she's about a hundred and fifty feet down."

"We have to hurry," said Austin, lowering himself onto the elevator track and climbing a scaffold similar to a widely rung ladder. An old prayer came back to him.

Yea, though I walk through the valley of the shadow of death, I will fear no evil.

He didn't know if God was telling him to be fearless or if he was about to die.

I guess it doesn't matter.

Cowboy was right behind him, and they executed the first switch. Cassidy was below them, blowing from side to side in the harsh wind.

The men moved as quickly as they could, executing several switches without incident when suddenly Austin fell. A rung was slippery with thick grease, and he plummeted twenty feet before slamming to a stop and crashing into the steel structure. He was too high on adrenaline to feel any pain. "Grease," he warned Cowboy, their shoes now slippery, making the descent more dangerous.

"Austin," Cassidy called.

"I'm coming." He couldn't look at her, needing total focus on every movement he made. It wasn't until the final switch that he dared lift his head, his heart in his throat. There with the city of Seattle and Elliott Bay in the background hung the woman he loved.

Their relationship flashed through his mind in its

entirety. The amazing weeks they'd shared all those years ago and what a fool he'd been to let her go. The picture her mother had pushed across the HERO Force conference table like a punch to the gut. Making love to Cassidy here, there, and everywhere, the way his soul felt melting with hers.

And now he could lose her.

He saw how precarious her grip was on the steel rope. She had no harness like he did—she simply had a loop around her torso like a lasso on a colt.

It must hurt like hell.

He imagined the cable digging into her skin and forced the image from his mind. He couldn't function if he thought of her like that. Couldn't stand it.

He unhooked his carabiner and braced himself on Cowboy, just as a tremendous wind caught his body and pushed him away from the steel. Cowboy grunted with the effort it took, but he held on, slowly pulling Austin back around, his feet gaining purchase.

Austin finally hooked onto the last eye in the steel he would need to descend. "Send down the hose!" he yelled as loudly as he could.

Cassidy's voice was weak and trembling. "I don't know much longer I can hang on. I love you..."

"Don't give up. Do you hear me?" he yelled. "You hang on and you don't give up."

"I'll try."

"Don't try. Do it."

She nodded.

The hose made it down to Cowboy and he wrapped it around and through Austin's harness, securing it with a thick knot. "The metal fitting will help hold it in place."

Austin took two more steps down before the hose tightened enough to support his weight. His stomach flip-flopped at the thought of what he had to do next. He pushed off the Space Needle and lunged for Cassidy, grabbing her by the waist.

The crowd down below went crazy, but she was still attached to the cable line and it snagged her backward, out of his grip. She nearly fell.

"Again," Austin called. "This time I'll grab you lower. Lift your arms and let the cable slide over your head."

Her face crumpled. "I'm scared."

"I won't let anything happen to you, Cassidy. I love you."

She nodded her head. "Ready."

He pushed off the tower again, grabbing her lower torso. She lifted her arms and the cable flew free.

"Hang on tight! We're going to hit the tower." He turned his body so he took the direct hit. Cowboy steadied them. The sound of a metal whip cut through the air as the cable she'd been hanging from dropped to the ground.

Cowboy lifted his head to the officers above. "Lower it down," he called. The firehose moved slowly and Cassidy buried her head in the crook of his neck.

"You're okay now," Austin cooed. His eyes met Cowboy's over Cassidy's shoulder. They weren't out of the woods just yet, and they both knew it.

Their feet hit the ground and reporters swarmed them. "Out of the way," Austin belted and the sea of people parted before him. He made his way back into the building with Cassidy right behind him.

The officer in charge met Austin's stare.

Something was terribly wrong. "What is it?"

"He got away."

"How the *fuck*?"

"Hang glider off the top of the needle. Must have been one of those folding models."

Fly like an angel.

Austin smacked his hand on the wall. "Son of a bitch."

"You need to leave the building," said the officer. "Bomb squad thinks they got all the explosives, but we need to clear the building just in case."

The group walked outside, again avoiding the press. When they made their way out of the crowd, Austin saw Noah walking toward them in the distance, his sniper rifle case hung over his shoulder.

"He fucking got away," said Austin.

Noah frowned. "You don't say?"

"Why you got your rifle?"

"Huntin' ducks."

Austin looked to Cassidy, who seemed as perplexed as he.

"Got me a big yellow one, flew right off the top of the Space Needle," said Noah. He grinned widely.

"You got him?" asked Austin.

Noah nodded. "Seattle's finest had the firehose secure without me. I came down here and got my rifle. The coast guard can fish him out of the Elliott Bay any time now."

24

Cassidy gingerly folded her hands in her lap, the gashes beneath her arms from the metal cable now stitched and bandaged, but terribly sore. She stole a glance at Austin.

He was driving them to a hotel. She didn't know where he got the car and she didn't care. He'd cleaned up at the hospital, the familiar spicy scent of him making her feel safe.

She'd been so sure she was going to die.

She'd even made her peace with it, hanging in the sky. She didn't want to die yet, but she was grateful for the life she'd had.

Grateful for Austin.

The love in her heart was the greatest gift of all, but as the surreal quality of the last few days began to lift like a heavy fog dispersing, she wondered if his declaration of love had more in common with a deathbed confession.

People wouldn't confess to the stuff they did if they knew they had to live with themselves afterward, and maybe—

just maybe—Austin wouldn't have said he loved her if he knew they'd be okay.

They reached the hotel, her weary legs trembling as she walked until Austin realized she was in pain and carried her. She wanted to cry then, the tears coming quickly and soaking into his shirt.

He kissed the top of her head.

She spent the whole night asleep in his arms. After their ordeal, it was all she wanted to do—the safest place in the world to combat the closest to death she had ever come.

She awoke once during the night, grateful for his strong arms around her, her eyes tracing the lines of his Navy SEAL insignia tattoo. She never expected Austin to come back into her life and she certainly never expected it would be her father to invite him here. She'd said as much to Austin as she was falling asleep in his arms, babbling from sheer exhaustion. "Maybe you two can get along after all."

Austin hadn't answered.

She tried not to read too much into that.

Hours later when she finally awoke, it was to the lazy sensation of Austin stroking her skin from her scalp to her ankles, desire for this man filled her like warm pudding in a cup. He kissed her skin beside her wounds. "I'm so sorry."

"You saved me."

She was at his mercy. She always had been, and she feared he would leave her again. They had no reason to stay together. David Kelleher was dead, Julianne was safe and Austin's assignment had been completed.

But she wasn't ready to let him go. Not now, not ever.

His touch became more sensual, his focus centered on her breasts. Then he was kissing them, tasting them with his tongue, the gentle motion and erotic thought of him there making her desperate for more. He sucked one nipple deep into his mouth.

He moved down her body and she wantonly spread her legs beneath his kisses, his tongue finding her most sensitive spot. His fingers slipped inside her, stroking and caressing, sliding in and out.

She cried out as she crested the wave of sensation, but still he touched and licked and kissed her as if he could never get enough. She came again as he entered her, lifting her ankles and resting them on his shoulders so that he filled her completely with his very first thrust.

She was flying, the ordeal she's been through only making the sensations sweeter. He squeezed one breast in his hand as he drove into her.

"Look at me," he commanded. She opened her eyes.

"I love you," he said, his thumb slipping between her folds to pleasure her. "I've always loved you."

Happiness filled her at his words. "I was so afraid you were going to leave."

"Never again. Not unless you want me to."

"I love you too."

He thrust into her harder, increasing his tempo, and her body convulsed around his shaft. He linked his hands with hers as his orgasm overtook him, moans of ecstasy rising up from his chest.

Cassidy smiled into the darkness as he came, wondering if she'd ever felt so happy or so loved. Austin was going to stay.

25

The sunshine seemed brighter as Cassidy made her way down the hotel hallway to Julianne's room. After so many days spent worrying for her friend, she was finally going to have a chance to throw her arms around Julianne and hug her tightly.

Maybe even cry a little. Or just talk.

The other woman had been through so much, even being hospitalized for two days after her rescue from The Community. She'd been raped regularly and would need ongoing counseling to deal with the emotional affects of that abuse.

Cassidy set her jaw as she did whenever she thought of Thomas. While she wished she'd never had to take a life, she wasn't sorry she'd killed him. She was only grateful she'd had the knife when she'd needed it.

She wondered what would happen to the members of The Community now. David, Thomas and Lucas were all dead. Would they return home to loved ones who thought they'd never see them again, welcomed back with open arms, or would they struggle to find their way in a world where David Kelleher was a madman and their home was no longer their own?

She sincerely hoped it was the first scenario, just as she hoped Julianne would be able to return to the life she'd had before she'd gone to The Community. She'd texted Cassidy to tell her the baby was doing okay and she couldn't wait to get back to her old life as soon as possible, yet Cassidy was sure there'd be a long road ahead.

Cassidy went to knock on the door of Julianne's room, but realized the metal piece had been swung out from the inside lock and was holding it open. She knocked anyway.

No answer. She rapped on it again, this time pushing the door open as she did. "Julianne?"

Julianne was probably sleeping, though she'd be sure to lecture her friend on making sure the door was locked before napping. Given her pregnancy and everything she'd been through it was easy to imagine she'd be profoundly tired.

The room was empty.

Cassidy spun in a circle. It barely even looked like she'd checked in. A paper on the desk caught her attention and she stepped to it. It wasn't in Julianne's handwriting, and a chill swept over Cassidy's skin as she read.

"I can't do this anymore. I hope you can forgive me."

Panic was instantaneous. She'd wildly underestimated her friend's struggle and now Julianne was going to kill herself. She'd left the door open on purpose, wanting her to find this.

Could it be a cry for help? Or was it truly the last thing she left behind?

She walked out of the room, not knowing what to do. She dialed Austin and told him about the note. Her eyes focused on the sign on the door in front of her.

STAIRS

ROOF ACCESS

"The roof," she said into the phone. "I have to check the roof."

"I'll be right there," he said.

She climbed up three flights of stairs, her legs no longer hurting from her hike up the Space Needle, and burst onto the rooftop, the sunlight blindingly bright.

"No!" The piercing scream could be heard from the other side of the rooftop condenser and she ran to it.

Cassidy rounded the corner to find her father with his back to her, Julianne awkwardly in his arms with her back to a half-wall that surrounded the rooftop. "Daddy?"

He turned abruptly to face her, giving Cassidy her first view of Julianne's face. She was sobbing.

Cassidy's mind worked to make sense of exactly what she was seeing. Her father's hands were on Julianne's shoulders, his grip apparently tight. "What the hell's going on?"

"He's trying to kill me! He doesn't want anyone to know about the baby," Julianne yelled.

Cassidy's mouth opened wide.

Her father stammered. "I'm not trying to kill you. I saved you. You were about to jump."

"Daddy?" she asked, so confused.

"It's all right now, sweetheart," he said.

Julianne wrestled her way out of the senator's grip, walking toward Cassidy. The truth that had been eluding her was suddenly clear. "The baby is my father's?"

"I'm so sorry," said Julianne.

"I can't believe this is happening."

Austin's voice boomed from behind her. "Tell her the rest, Senator Lane."

He shrugged, still standing close to the wall. "There's nothing to tell. It happened one time, that's all."

Julianne pointed at him. "A year and a half. He told me he was getting a divorce. Then when I wouldn't have an abortion he got angry."

Austin walked past Cassidy, heading straight for the senator. "Tell them the rest, I said. Tell them what you said to David Kelleher."

The senator said nothing. Austin got within a foot of his face. "You knew what would happen if Julianne's cover at The Community was exposed. She was in a dangerous position. If Kelleher found out she was a reporter her very life would be in danger."

The senator shook his head. "It wasn't me."

Julianne marched toward him, shoving him in the chest. "You were the one who did this to me? How could you?"

"I didn't. I mean, I didn't know," he said.

"You didn't know what? That they would torture me? That I'd be raped every day?"

The first trace of emotion showed on his face and he covered his mouth just as quickly.

She pushed him again. "You would have had me die because I wouldn't kill your child!"

He was backed against the wall, his jaw trembling. He looked from one person to the next and back again. "I...I..." He turned abruptly, then turned and put his knee on the wall.

"Daddy!" screamed Cassidy.

Austin grabbed him before he could go over, yanking him back from certain death to face him. "To think, I used to want to be good enough for you," said Austin. "I'm more of a man than you'll ever be."

26

S ometimes heroes fall from grace.

The first hero Cassidy ever had in her life wasn't Austin. It was her father. Watching his public disgrace—his arrest, the mugshots on the nightly news, the complete implosion of his marriage—was very nearly more than she could bear.

She knew he was guilty. There was no question. But that didn't make it any easier to handle.

The fact that all of it came mere hours after she and Austin had professed their love made it that much more difficult. It was hard to love the one man her father hated at a time when her father was going through so much.

Yes, he brought it on himself. But she'd made a decision after all the cards had been played not to abandon him completely, and that was what she was trying very hard to do. But no matter which way she leaned on any given day—more toward Austin or more toward her father—she was being disloyal to someone involved.

Someone she loved.

And it was tearing her apart.

She told herself she should let her father go. He was clearly the one who deserved it, but she couldn't bring herself to do it. She was literally all he had left in the world.

Her father thought her relationship with Austin showed how much she hated him, while Austin thought her relationship with her father showed she was certifiably insane.

She'd told herself it was the stress of the moment that had made everything seem so intense with Austin, that it wasn't real, just a dream.

It gave her an out so she could stop hurting.

And if she missed him when she went to sleep and when she woke up and every moment in between, it was because it had been a tough year and not because he was meant to be in her life.

The day she finally broke it off with Austin, she'd packed up the meager belongings she'd purchased since coming to Atlanta straight from Idaho (what had she been thinking?) and waited until he came home from work.

He stopped two steps inside the door, looking from her to the suitcase before throwing his keys down on the table. "You're leaving?"

She nodded.

He could have been a statue, he was so still. The moment stretched out into an awkward silence. She moved to him, went on her tiptoes and kissed his cheek. "I can't do this anymore."

He didn't say anything. He didn't even turn his head as she pulled her suitcase behind her and walked out the door.

She still couldn't believe how easily he'd let her go.

Really? You can't believe it?

He knew how much it was hurting you. What was he supposed to do, beg you to stay?

She'd moved back to D.C. like she'd hardly even been

away. A little vacation, that's all. A month that nearly cost her her life, then took all the joy out of living.

It was better this way.

There was nothing else she could do.

27

Cassidy finished typing and let her hands drop to her sides. The office sounds around her were surreal, as if she'd been on a trip through time that had only affected her.

On her screen were twenty thousand words that rehashed the most difficult year of her life. Her time in The Community. Her near death experience dangling from the Seattle Space Needle. Her father's arrest and public humiliation.

Austin was in it, too. She needed the piece to be an authentic representation of that time in her life and that couldn't be so if she left him out. Besides, the *Post* had run a photo of her in Austin's arms when they hit the ground, the photographer catching a moment of such intense intimate feeling, it was useless to deny there had been a relationship.

Her editor walked into her cubicle and sat. He was a tall skinny man with deep brown skin who'd been more of a father to her this past year than her own would ever be again. "Julianne had the baby?" he asked.

Cassidy grinned, the memory of her sweet little half-brother's birth still fresh in her mind. It had taken some time, but Cassidy and Julianne had repaired their friendship. Cassidy was making every effort to embrace this new part of her family instead of pushing them away. "Six pounds, four ounces. She named him Charlie."

"Aww. Tell her to bring him around sometime. And if she decides she wants her job back, she's just got to say the word."

"Thanks, Derek. I'll let her know."

He looked pointedly at her laptop. "Did you get to the end?"

"I did."

"And do you hate it?"

The piece she had written was like the ugliest part of her soul smeared on canvas. "I do."

"Then it's honest and true. Probably win a damn Pulitzer."

She laughed, her eyes watering with unshed tears. "I wouldn't relive this year again if you paid me."

"Does she get the SEAL in the end?"

She shook her head, her fight to keep her tears in check no longer even a question. "It wasn't meant to be."

"Good. The Pulitzer judges hate happy endings."

She laughed begrudgingly. "Fuck you, Derek."

"Tell me something, princess. If I read the rest of what you've written there, will I want you to end up with that man?"

"Probably."

"And if you could write the ending any way you wanted to, would you want the two of you to end up together?"

"Probably." She wiped at her cheek. "But it's not fiction. It's reality."

"It's your story, Cassidy. It may be reality, but you get to write the ending." He stood up and smacked a rolled-up newspaper on her desk before leaving.

She reread the last few paragraphs, which now seemed like a pathetic attempt to wrap something ugly up tight with a bow. She saved her progress and closed the computer, packing up her things to go home.

By the time she got to her car she knew she didn't want to go home.

She pulled out her cell phone, searching for Austin in her contacts, but it wasn't a phone call she wanted with strained conversation and long distance apologies. She wanted Austin, right in front of her face.

Instead she dialed Cowboy, who'd become a fast friend during her time in Atlanta. "Are you guys in town?"

"I'm flattered, but I'm kind of seeing somebody."

"Leo," she laughed.

"Oh, you want Austin!" he feigned surprise. "He came in last night. Should be home, far as I know."

"Thank you."

"Anytime, sweetheart. I was hoping you'd call."

She hung up, exhaling dramatically and dropping her shoulders before opening her browser and looking for a flight.

Derek was right. Her life wasn't something that happened to her. She made it happen, and she wasn't willing to settle for the way things had ended between her and Austin.

The piece she wrote for the *Post* put it all in perspective and allowed her to flush all the aching and turmoil from her system, leaving only a weary acceptance and a loneliness she wouldn't name until Derek did it for her.

She missed Austin.

It was nine-fifteen the next morning when Atlanta appeared on the horizon, almost ten when she rang his bell.

She was certain he'd be glad to see her until she was in the air hurtling toward him through the sky, but she forced her fears to a tiny corner of her mind and locked them in there. The cab dropped her off at his condo.

I hope I didn't screw this one up forever.

She rang the bell. He answered the door in sweatpants and nothing else, his hair tossed from sleep and his eyes boring holes into hers.

"Cowboy said you'd be home."

He nodded. "Here I am."

"I'm sorry, Austin."

He pulled her into his arms and held her tightly, it was as if not a moment had passed since she knew she was in love with him, and she promised herself not another moment would go by without him in her life.

"I missed you so much," he whispered into her neck. "I'm sorry I made it so hard for you to love me. That I wanted you to choose between me and your father. I won't do it again."

She shushed him and kissed his mouth. Their first kiss was gentle and poignant. Their second was full of lust.

There'd already been too much talking. All she wanted to do now was show him how much he meant to her, to share her body with him and hold him tightly inside her.

Austin pulled her shirt over her head with one hand and slammed the door shut with the other.

She was home.

28

Cassidy stood with her back to Austin, staring at the river, the rolling autumn fields and the snow-covered mountains in the distance. "I love Colorado. It's so beautiful."

They'd been dating for seven months. She'd moved to Atlanta just weeks after her impromptu trip—bringing her things this time—and settling into his life and his home like she simply belonged there.

He moved closer to her back, wrapping his arms around her midsection and kissing her neck. "I have something special planned for today."

She giggled. "Like yesterday when you wouldn't let me leave the bed? That was pretty special."

"This is more outdoorsy."

She spun around in his arms. "Can we be naked?"

He laughed and she loved the sound of it, the deep tenor making her smile. She was kidding about being naked, but if he asked her to, she most certainly would oblige.

"If you're lucky." He winked. "Come on."

He led her along a hiking trail dripping with vibrant fall

foliage, the scent of fall heavy on the air and woodsmoke in the distance.

These past months had been more than Cassidy could have hoped for. All the stress that had led her to breakup with Austin was gone, with only understanding in its wake. He even drove with her to visit her father, knowing all the while she didn't want him to come inside.

He just wanted to be there for her.

Austin's constant traveling was hard to get used to, but now that she'd gotten a job at the *Atlanta Journal-Constitution*, she was engrossed in her own work and loving it.

The other members of HERO Force had really welcomed her into their little family, with Charlotte being Cassidy's favorite. She was fun and fearless and a true match for Cowboy, not to mention amazingly good at karaoke on their weekly girls' night out.

"Thanks for bringing me here," she said. "I like my surprise."

"This isn't it."

"No?"

He shook his head. "It's up there, just past that bend in the trail."

She rounded the corner and gasped. A ten-foot pool of crystal blue water steamed in the cool autumn air. It was surrounded by boulders, a small stream coming out of the spring and trickling along the forest floor. "Oh, wow."

"It's a hot spring. We can swim in it."

"Really? But I didn't bring my suit." She reached down to feel the water, moaning at the luxuriously warm temperature. "It's like bath water."

He took off his sweatshirt and T-shirt beneath. "You're the one who wanted to get naked."

Her eyes widened. "What if somebody sees us?"

"It just adds to the fun." He walked to her and untucked her shirt from her pants.

"You're serious."

"Hell yeah, I'm serious."

She looked around. They hadn't seen anyone else on their hike so far, but that didn't mean that would continue. She watched Austin as he continued to undress, her eyes fixed on the bulge in his pants as he took off his belt.

"You stare at me, I get to stare at you," he said.

She licked her lips. "Sounds fair." She pulled her shirt over her head, the cool air and Austin's heated gaze instantly hardening her nipples. He released the clasp on her bra and let it drop to the ground.

"All of it," he said.

The air was cold on his warm skin but she wanted to remember this moment forever, to memorize the beautiful lines of his body against the beautiful backdrop of nature.

She unfastened her jeans and pushed them down her legs, realizing she hadn't taken off her hiking boots. She burst out laughing.

Austin crossed to her and kneeled down. "Let me help." He untied her laces and helped her slip the shoes off, then kissed her legs, letting his hands stroke between them. When he pulled her panties down, she reached down and pulled Austin back up, hungrily kissing his mouth.

He still had clothes on and she worked to get them off him before leading him into the very warm water.

"It's like a hot tub," she said, awe in her voice. She touched one of the boulders that sat half in the water. "Feel these rocks. They're warm."

He crossed to her, cupping her breasts instead. "Very warm."

"You got any warm rocks for me to feel?" she asked playfully, her hand finding his balls and kneading them gently. She stroked his hardening cock. "Oh, here's a really big rock..."

He captured her mouth in a kiss, teasing her with his tongue. She wrapped her legs around his waist and guided his cock inside her. He groaned with the sensation of her body clutching him tightly.

Austin had never been loved like this.

Not the sex, though the sex was amazing. He'd never been loved like he was loved by Cassidy. He'd been biding his time, waiting for things with her family to settle down, waiting for her to get a new job, waiting for every little domino to line up in a row so he could knock them all down in one all-consuming stunt, and it was finally time to ask her.

Her eyes were closing, her body pumping up and down on his, and he reclined on a rock, letting her take control of their lovemaking. He watched her cheeks flush, the rosy pink color that painted her neck and chest, the hard little nubs of her nipples.

She was loud when she came, her voice echoing off the trees, and he took hold her hips, driving into her body at his pace now. Her orgasm continued, her muscles sucking him until he went over the edge into oblivion.

Their breathing slowed. He settled backwards again, taking her with him. He reached into his pants pocket and pulled out the ring, fitting it on the first knuckle of his index finger and tucking her under the chin.

"Mmm," she said lethargically.

"Wake up, sleepyhead."

"Mmm."

He kissed her forehead. "I could spend every day of my life like this with you."

"I'm not moving to Colorado," she deadpanned.

He laughed. "It's not the place. It's the person. I love you, Cassidy."

"Love you, too."

"Marry me."

She sat up abruptly. "What?"

He reached for his pants and dug in the pocket for the small box he kept there. He held out the ring, never more nervous in his life than he was in that moment, and that included all his time in the military. "Marry me. Be my wife."

She took the ring, concern taking over her features. "But I don't cook."

He laughed. "So what?"

"Don't you want a woman who makes cookies and hosts recipe exchanges. That's not who I am. That's not somebody I'm ever going to be."

He narrowed his eyes. "What makes you think I care so much about food?"

"Your mom makes bread from scratch. I interview gangsters. Sometimes I don't even wash my clothes."

He cocked his head. "Am I missing something? I don't want to marry my mother, Cassidy. I want to marry you. And if you're happy being an investigative reporter with dirty jeans, then I'm happy with you just the way you are."

"Really?"

"Yes. Where did you get this crazy idea from?"

"Your mother told me, when you took me to meet your family."

"Ahh... She has a funny sense of humor. It takes some getting used to."

Cassidy's eyes went wide. "That was a joke?"

"Yeah. She told my high school girlfriend I was gay. Something about if it's meant to be, it will survive any obstacle."

"That's horrible! I'm going to kill her."

"Can you wait until she's your mother-in-law?"

She shook her head vigorously. "Yes." She put one hand on either side of his face and kissed him. "I love you so much, Austin." She laughed, squeezing him tightly.

"Twice in my life I thought I'd lost you," he said. "Promise me you won't let us drift apart like we did when things get tough. Promise me you'll hang on to me even tighter."

Her throat was thick with emotion and she worked to get the words past it. "I promise. I won't let you go. Not ever again."

NOAH NEEDS THE ONE THING THAT ISN'T IN HIS BUG-OUT BAG. HANNAH FIELDING.

Buy Kidnapped by the SEAL

Sign up for Amy Gamet's mailing list
or text BOOKS to 66866

A note from the author

PLEASE TAKE a moment to leave a review. Writing is solitary work, and feedback from readers puts a smile on my face and helps to counteract things like my kids calling me "the fun ender" and having to do laundry. (I really hate laundry.)

If you're reading on a kindle, note that the "rate this book" feature at the end of an book is not the same as leaving a review. Only Amazon sees those ratings and the stars have no effect on the star rating of the book.

The number of reviews and their star-rating determine

where I can advertise and promote my books. They also help other readers make purchasing decisions.

This link will take you back to write a review at the retailer where you bought this book. Thank you so much for taking the time!

All the best,

Amy Gamet

Made in the USA
Coppell, TX
27 September 2024

37761016R00090